The Moon & othe

Written by various autho

Edited by David Heyman

Published by Synthetic Minds Press 2020

Copyright © Synthetic Minds Press & Respective authors of the individual works included.

The authors have asserted their right under the Copyright, Designs and Patents act of 1988 to be identified as the authors of this work

No part of this book may be copied or shared without prior written consent from the author or authors.

All people, places and events mentioned in this book are fictitious, any resemblance to the real is both terrifying and coincidental.

Table of contents

Title	Page
The Moon by C.S.R Thomas	**4**
The Moor of McCallahan by C.S.R Thomas	**17**
About C.S.R Thomas	**22**
The Sea Versus James Jonah Monroe by Martha Jones	**23**
About Martha Jones	**50**
Selene by Georg Isen	**51**
About Georg Isen	**81**
Urgent Tortoise By Richard Owen Collins	**82**
About Richard Owen Collins	**109**
Grey Gunge By Rob Lang	**110**
About Rob Lang	**147**
Notes from an Innarian Ecologist By David Heyman	**148**
About David Heyman	**171**

About this book

The Moon & Other Tales is the result of a number of authors very generously donating their time and creativity in response to the many issues and crises occurring across our planet. While it may feel impossible at times to do anything to help, by purchasing this book you have already made a difference. All money made from this collection, minus the sales tax taken by Amazon, is directly donated to charitable action.

We have chosen to support the Nature Conservancy Australia because we believe their work is vital in the face of the devastating fires that spread through Australia in 2019. However, given the nature of their work, we believe they also have a significant impact across the world meaning the money given will ultimately help us all.

Thank you for supporting us and them.

The Moon
By C.S.R Thomas

I was born on the colony.

One of the first, so I suppose in a way I was just another experiment— the son of the Project Director and the Head of Cryoresearch.

I played with the few friends that I could find. I went to an advanced school for the advanced children of advanced minds and all the while I dreamt.

I dreamt of the blue and green orb that hung in the sky. I read about it, fiction and facts. There was another world up there. A world of billions. People of a hundred hues, beliefs, passions and fears. A world of many varied species of beasts; massive and small, peaceful and deadly and everything in between. A world of space and freedom, of hope and passion and of wonder and excitement. The adults called it that Old Rock, but I loved it.

Beyond the windows of the habitat I called home there was just a featureless grey expanse, but in my mind's eye, I could see rolling green fields under a soft blue sky. I could see rivers and forests and vast oceans. All full of life.

The greatest variety of life here was in the bio-labs. Plants and animals were kept there for experimentation and analysis; tiny microcosms of Earth's different habitats. But I treasured every time that they let me tour those rooms, seeing what new specimens they'd received and gleefully reciting every little detail I could recall about them.

Most lived in bio-domes. Micro-environments maintained to investigate their utility for producing food, oxygen and energy for colonies on other worlds. A lot of our work supported the much larger colonies on Mars, which were still under construction. I didn't care about that... all I knew is that they were small slices of what the real Earth had to offer. I would lie down on the soft grass, close my eyes and listen to the sounds of the world I had never known. The buzzing of insects, the rustling of plants against the air-ducts and, best of all, the birdsong. But behind it there was always the hum of our generators, the sliding of mechanical doors and the chattering of busy scientists. When I opened my eyes and looked up I didn't see a vast, blue sky but a sun-lamp adorned silver ceiling.

The other children were nice enough, I suppose. We were all from varied backgrounds, so there weren't enough similarities for anyone difference to stand out. All different colours, accents, faiths and philosophies… nobody could pick on anyone else without making themselves a target. That was nice, in a way. But the biggest difference, I suppose, was me. I was the oldest, but I was also the only one who really loved the Old Rock. The others were intrigued by some aspects of it but spent more time just mocking the Earthers.

We were special. We were clearly so much better than all those slack-jawed, stupid little kids on the earth below us. They were the past. We were the future, and nothing quite unites a group like hate. It seemed best for me to keep my hobbies to myself, but even then, I always felt like an outsider, though I was never directly treated as one. Their interests were all so serious and scientific, directed mainly by whatever fields their parents worked in. I mean, I helped my father out with the cryo research a lot, but I also found the time to relax and to indulge my passions. None of the others ever seemed to just be kids! To have some fun! But I suppose I only knew what they did when we were all together... maybe, in private, they had their own secret indulgences. Perhaps they were just like me.

Never really got the chance to find out.
The adults were a different matter. They were all from different parts of Earth as well, but they hadn't grown up together like we had. There were so many little rivalries and biases based on past feuds. It seemed silly to us. Stuff like that shouldn't matter up here. Even I agreed that baggage like that belonged back on the Old Rock.

This was all normally just harmless stuff; a tendency for the adults to form cliques and perhaps the odd joke here and there, but there was one particularly important divide that seemed a lot more dangerous. Two of the nations that funded the Colony had been rivals, fighting in every way but all-out war. The UN mainly organised the colony. Inviting both of the feuding nations to participate was to be an olive-branch between them; an acknowledgement that they could do much more together than apart. But there were still people who held onto the old grudges. They worried about one side having too much influence on the colonies and turning them into yet more territories for their homeland.

  News from Earth always showed the leaders of the two Great Nations acting nice to each other. They behaved like considerate allies on the surface, pretending nothing was going behind the scenes. They smiled through gritted teeth and shook one another's' hands. But every debate would see them on opposing sides, politely detailing why the other's stance was flawed and inherently wrong. Pointed criticisms and hypothetical threats were tossed around like bullets and bombs. Eventually, it reached a peak. I was only 14. One Nation accused the other Nation of hoarding certain materials utilised in the construction of a particularly devastating weapon. The other Nation refuted such claims citing the first Nations tight (and, dare they suggest, potentially unlawful) control of said restricted materials. These points were all made with the utmost politeness but with a firm indication that the Nation presenting the points would pursue the matter for the protection of all the countries of Earth. Very stirring. Very heroic. It certainly spoke to the patriots in the colony's staff. Over 40% of them returned to earth following the debates. Some wanted to help defend their people in the event of a conflict. Some were recalled by their government; "Your country has need of you." That was the last time I saw my father.

    My mother told me that soon the politicians posturing would end. That the UN would investigate the claims of both sides, deal with any offences directly, and we could return to focusing on the future. Their countries had been like this for generations, and they both had enemies other than each other. If they focused too much on their rivalries they'd be defenceless against other threats. Soon it would all go back to normal again, and everyone could return home. She told me not to worry about my Dad.

The truth is; I wasn't. I wasn't worried about him at all. I was jealous. He was on Earth, and I wasn't. He'd have something different to eat every day. He'd wake up to birdsong and rain. I wanted to be down there with him feeling the wind on my skin in a city full of strangers. I remember going out to the Viewing Deck and staring up at that beautiful blue Old Rock, nothing between us but glass and void. My Dad was up there somewhere and I'd have given anything to be there with him. And that was when I saw the first light.

    It was a speck of orange where there shouldn't be one, just the tiniest little glint at first, somewhere in Europe. The swirls of clouds seemed to retreat from it, forming a ring of grey tendrils around the glare. It was just a small dot, but I felt a cold lump in my stomach at the thought of how huge it must have been to be visible to my naked eye. I recoiled, taking a step towards the door, I knew I should get someone, tell them something horrible was happening! But for that moment I was frozen, and in just a second the hateful little pustule burst into a blackness that seeped out into the spiralling cloud, spreading out like a dark bruise. As I stared, I saw another speck of light flare up, to the north of the original. And then another, somewhere in the Americas. And another… and another…

Tears were streaming down my face by the time I realised I was no longer alone. My mother had come out to join me. I'd been gone for almost an hour and she'd been worried, but when she saw what was happening on the world above she fell silent. At least eight lights had flared up and burst by now. The choking tendrils of black clouds met and intermingled, fattening out to obscure the features of the old rock. Eventually, others came. Apparently, all broadcasts from earth had suddenly stopped; they were wondering what was going on. When they saw what was happening they rushed back to comms, desperately trying to contact someone, anyone, on earth. There was no response. Eventually, they came back and just stood with us, staring up at a world that was now covered over half its surface by a choking black fog. I'm not sure how many lights there were in the end. Occasionally we'd see the muted glare of one from within the murk, followed by a bulge in the clouds and a lurching increase of its growth. We all stood there, for hours, until the last speck of blue was devoured by that darkness. Together we watched the world die.

Over the next few weeks we tried, constantly, day and night, to make contact with Earth. There was no response. We couldn't pick up any signals at all. We had no idea if the cloud was blocking them or if there was simply no-one and nothing left to hear.

The cloud itself had grown lighter and thinner. It was a sickly brown, and after a few days, we began to be able to make out the occasional contours of the larger landmasses. What little glimpses we had did not inspire hope. The day I spied a sickly yellow through a crack in the clouds and realised I was looking at what had once been the ocean I cried and thought I'd never stop. Eventually, it was decided that we had no option left to us but to attempt to find out what the situation was for ourselves. It wasn't difficult for the more technologically adept of our number to jury rig a dozen automated devices, designed to drop beneath the cloud, take some scans, then boost back up and re-establish a signal to us while travelling a few kilometres off to try again. They measured toxicity and radiation levels, but primarily we were looking for life readings or signs of energy generation and consumption. We were hoping for survivors.

There was some life down there, but it was widely scattered. It was weak, and on occasion, it was unidentifiable. If there were any humans left down there then they were too few for the scouts to have spotted them. From the readings we were getting it seemed that the poisonous climate that had enveloped the earth was going to get worse long before it got better. At least a century before it started fading away and centuries more before a human could breathe the air unsupported again. You'd have better luck surviving on Venus. The Earth we knew, the Earth I loved, was gone. At first, people didn't accept it. They were certain that somewhere down there there must be someone still alive; that the scouts would send back a report showing somewhere underground still generating and utilising energy or an area where the toxic miasma was weak enough for people to survive. Eventually, the scouts ran out of fuel and one by one they stopped making their daily reports. Some people wanted to recall the ones that had not yet died, to continue the search. But my mother and the other project leads declined. They said we'd need the fuel. They had a plan: the Martian Colonies. They were uncompleted, over half their infrastructures would still be completely uninhabitable. But they were larger than the Lunar Colony; their supply stocks would last for longer and, most importantly; they had people. The construction work there required a small army of people filling a variety of roles; basic engineers, robotics experts, architects and scientists… Even a few test families. The last humans.

They told us this was the last hope for humanity. The Mars Colony could survive on what it had for some time, but on its own they would not be able to complete construction, nor would they be able to establish renewable supplies of food and energy. But we could. We could take what we'd learnt here and build life anew there. We needed to take what we could from here, dismantle the rest and leave. We all needed to pull together for this, every last one of us.

My job was to assist in the salvaging of technology from the bio and cryo labs and to safely, swiftly and humanely dispose of any untransportable biomatter. My own mother gave me these orders.

We worked in silence most of the time. Either through depression or determination. We spoke little of our tasks and it didn't take long before we were all done. Packed up and prepared, ready to leave our home behind and make a new life on the red planet, the new homeworld of the human race. Few people smiled as we loaded up our transportation, those that did were forced and weak. The other children were scared of meeting other people, normal people. But it was what they had to do, it was what we had to do for the human race to survive. But our survival was not the one I was concerned about.

Being one of the remaining cryo-specialists, I was given the duty of securing the hibernation pods for one of the transports. I had to make sure every pod was safe, secure, and that the readings for the occupant were stable before initiating the automated course and sealing myself into the remaining pod. I did so carefully, assuring that every soul slumbering on that shuttle would wake up safely in their new life, I confirmed the course, I activated the automatic launch and made absolutely sure that the computer would not acknowledge the absence of a sleeper in the remaining pod.

I stepped off the shuttle, back into my home. It seemed large enough now that it was empty. The halls were already growing cold, and I had only an hour before life support wound down entirely. Just enough time to make sure the changes I made to the Biolabs were keeping the life there as perfectly preserved as the people on those shuttles, ready for eventual reintroduction.

And, of course, to tuck myself in for a long sleep.

The Moor of McCallahan
By C.S.R Thomas

Twas a tenebrous and squally night 'pon the Moor of McCallahan. Robbie Rattray was a'lurching his way homeward from a rambunctious, tumultuous evening down the local pub which bore the drawn-out moniker of "The Leg O' The Coo that Chud Ya".

The man was jolly and his insides were stewing merrily in the warm glow of inebriated Elysium, disregarding of the extreme chilly inclemency of his surroundings, but as his heavy leather boots sunk into the mushy, muddy marshlands he felt a pin-prick of frost strike the back of his neck.

He stopped dead in his tracks 'pon the marshy Moor of McCallahan and in that heinous moment his warm, safe fermentation forced its way from his form. He blinked slowly in the light of the few stars and the many moons and took in the tree line of jagged, wicked shadows in the distance.

He glanced down at the peat as it popped at him and let out the stench of drowned furry creatures who strayed too far upon this lands treacherous features.

The pin-prick 'pon his neck was like a dagger, gently touching 'tween the bumps of his spine. He had to run homeward, he had to run to the arms of his dearest lovely Laura… but his legs would nae move. A lot of good they'd have done him, for as has been intimated already the geography of the area was callous to those foolhardy of step, and the bog would have pounced 'pon the opportunity to suck his boot right of his feet, then take his tootsies next.

The lad was young and had no urge to let his life a'loose so lightly, so he took in the largest of breaths his Scot-borne lungs could handle and straightened his body up. He clenched his fists and slowly but surely moved his feet around to face the foreboding force that lurked behind him.

    And sure enough as he looked behind, he spied a horrifying Beastie! With thick white hair and blazing eyes which had young Robbie fixed squarely in their sights. The Beastie was at least twice as tall as Robbie was and twice as long as' twas tall, and Rob saw straight the cruel look of disdain it bore upon its brow.

He took a step backwards and the mean ol' Moor of McCallahan let out a bubbling laugh as it clutched at his boot and sucked it out from under the poor young man who tumbled backwards, his behind buried in the peat and marsh. He was looking straight up upon the Beasties facial features now, which were long and gaunt, tight to its bones and covered in a shorter pelt than the thick curly coat that adorned its body. Its eyes were black, cruel and cold-blooded. Above them were curling golden horns, that shimmered 'neath the moonlight and glinted at their pointed ends which poked straight towards young Robbie. Beneath the eyes the beasties nostrils flared and breathed a breath, visible in the cold nights' air, which crawled around Rob's face before dissipating. The Beastie took a sturdy, heavy step forwards towards our hero who let out his most valorous whimper and closed his eyes praying softly to whatever gods felt a young man inclined to debauchery and decadence was worthy of their mercies.

The Beast's face was inches from Robbie's now, and it's puffs of hot breath could be felt by him. Methodically and with great consideration the Beastie narrowed it's ebon eyes and dragged it's long soused and sodden tongue from Rob's chin up to his brow. The drool of the demonic Beastie mingled with the sweat and tears borne from Rob's own panic and with that the Beastie turned slowly around. It seemed to Rob to take a lifetime for the Beastie to have completed its 180-degree rotation, but he thanked whichever gods had answered him when it had, and when it began to stride off back into the haze of the Moor of McCallahan.

    Rob slowly picked himself up, and abandoning his lost shoe for the Moor of McCallahan is a covetous creature, began to continue his way homeward back into the loving arms of his dear Laura.

He gave no thought to the beasties intentions of that night, he gave no thought to the meaning in its tongues molestation of his features.

He gave no thought to the slightly burning mark on his forward, which stung for a few minutes then melted away.

He gave no thought to the changes he felt in his form, the bumps he felt 'pon his brow, the curly fur he felt growing 'pon his arms, the primal voices he felt bleating in his brain.

Laura would get more'n she bargained for that night.
'pon the Moor of McCallahan.

About the author:

Celyn is a horrible goblin who spends his time playing too many games and writing too little. In his non-spare time he adults for people who can not adult despite not being capable of adulting for himself.

The Sea Versus James Jonah Monroe

By Martha Jones

Ages ago, man told the sea he would tame her, and she would one day serve him.

And the sea laughed.

Years rolled in and out with the tides, and the sea watched as man became many men.

Some men were clever, some were kind, some loved the sea with all their hearts, and some feared her so completely that they never left dry land.

An irksome few of these men were still convinced the sea should bow to them, not they to her. They built sturdy boats in which they ventured farther and farther from their homelands.

The sea couldn't help but admire these bold rascals and let most of them pass through her waters unharmed. The rest she sank pitilessly in her depths. And whenever the mood overtook her, she would send mermaids to greet presumptuous sailors as a warning that they had strayed out of their depths.

Many a sailor saw these mermaids and chose to journey forward, not back to where they'd come from. Those who lived long enough to tell the tale of what they'd seen were few enough in number that their fellow seafarers dismissed them outright.

"Some fish story," said they. "May all our captains be so generous with their rum rations."

Centuries ago, there lived a man called Captain Monroe. James Jonah Monroe was the slickest, greediest pirate captain west of the Irish Sea. His love of gold and ill-gotten goods overpowered his hate for the sea, and for seventeen years, this love had lured him away from land in search of treasure.

And Captain Monroe did hate the sea: the way she looked, the way she smelled, and the way she changed temperament without warning.

The sea didn't much care for Captain Monroe, either. Twice she had sunk the ships on which he sailed in effort to humble if not destroy him, and twice he had survived to spit curses at her from the shore.

One night, Captain Monroe was carousing and playing cards in a pub near the docks of Cape Fear. Mr Carter, his first mate and Mr Chapman, expert gunner and reluctant harpooner, watched as the captain attempted to cheat a fisherman in a game of cards. Mr Chapman sipped his pint and paid as much heed as ever he did to the captain while off duty. Mr Carter, on the other hand, was a rather good card player, and as he observed the game before them, noticed something remarkable.

"The fisherman's losing on purpose," he whispered to Mr Chapman, and pointed out several plays the captain ought to have lost, had the fisherman been playing his best.

"Do you think the captain knows?" Mr Chapman whispered back.

"I doubt he cares. He does so love to win," said Mr Carter.

"Any idea what the wager was?" asked Mr Chapman.

"A love-starved mule or mother-in-law, I should think," said Mr Carter.

After a thorough beating at the rummy table, the fisherman wagged his head said, "You're too smart for me, Capt'n. How much do I owe you, now?"

"Three pounds ten." said the captain, "Despite your less than lofty manner and apparel, I presume you have no intention of trying to cheat me?"

"None at all, Capt'n," said the fisherman. He lowered his eyes and clasped his hands together in a practiced kowtow. "I'm no beggar, and I too would be mighty upset if I thought I'd been swindled by the likes me. However, before I surrender your three pounds ten, might I try to tempt you with something a bit better? Something-- priceless?"

Captain Monroe said some crude words to the odious fisherman, but his two shipmates and he agreed to visit his home and see what-oh what- such a man would consider "priceless."

The fisherman led them to a crooked shack a little way from the pier and invited them inside. Though moonlight streamed through the door and the tiny window, it was not half enough to illuminate the shack's shabby interior, so the fisherman lit a lantern. Then, the three astonished sailors stood with jaws agape as they beheld on the floor in front of them a living, wild-eyed mermaid

"Lovely, isn't she?" said the fisherman in a hushed voice of wonder-gilded terror.

The mermaid was indeed lovely. Her hair was long and shimmering, green and gold like aged bronze in the flicker of the lamplight. Her tail was green as well but smooth one way and coarse the other, like the skin of a shark. Her dainty body and arms were bound in a jumble of twine and weatherworn nets.

"Can she breathe down there?" asked Mr Chapman, a trifle breathless, himself.

"Certainly she can breath," said the fisherman, "Merfolk don't need the water for breathin.' They're just stronger there. That's all."

The fisherman explained that he had been hard at work the day before pulling a heavy catch aboard his boat, and in his nets among the bass and snappers was the unhappy mermaid. The waves were high, and the sky was so dark that in his frantic row for the dock, he didn't even know she was there, only that he had caught something quite heavy.

"She must've hit her head when I jostled the nets because she lay still in the boat when I found her," said the fisherman. "Then, of course, I dared not put her back for fear of what the sea in her anger or the mermaid herself might do, so I dried her off and tied her up, and went lookin' for them what might be man enough to take her off my hands."

"So you gambled and lost to the captain so you could trick us into coming here," said Mr Carter, guessing this fisherman would have paid them to get rid of the mermaid for him, had he the means.

"Why the gag?" asked Mr Chapman upon seeing the mermaid's mouth full of rags.

"Have you not heard?" said the fisherman. "Mermaids bewitch the seafarin' man with their voices.

They sing 'em into stupors that make 'em dash their ships against the rocks."

Captain Monroe saw at once the fisherman was offering him a golden opportunity in this mermaid.

"With one of her own our prisoner, the sea wouldn't dare scuttle the ship," said Captain Monroe. Then, he shouted toward the harbor at the top of his voice, "You hear that? Just try to sink me again, Madam, and I'll fillet your daughter for my supper!"

The Captain hastily gathered a crew and provisions, then set sail from Cape Fear. For a whole week, Captain Monroe stood on deck taunting the waters to swallow them whole, to the uneasiness of everyone on board. But the waters remained at bay. The weather was bleak, and the waves were angry, but the aptly named Nemesis, Captain Monroe's ship, sailed through the waves unharmed. The captain now had no doubt that the fisherman had given him a grand talisman in the mermaid.

Emboldened beyond reason, Captain Monroe went below deck to visit the mermaid in a small closet near the galley's pantry where he had her stowed. He chose the galley because it was the most watertight part of the ship. Also, he wanted her there so she could plainly smell the cook's semi-eternal roasting of fish (for the captain meant what he said about making a meal of the mermaid should things not go the way he wanted).

Captain Monroe dismissed the cook and stepped inside the closet to have a word with his captive.

"Do you speak?" asked Captain Monroe.

The Mermaid nodded. The captain vowed to her he would bring her to slow, deliberate harm if she tried to bewitch him toward the rocks. The Mermaid nodded again, and Captain, Monroe untied the rags that bound her jaws.

"Your mother has taken a great deal of treasure from the ships of men," said Captain Monroe as he locked eyes with the mermaid.

"Surely you don't believe they deserved it more than she," said the mermaid in a voice both breathy and beguiling.

"I don't care who deserves it, Missy. I want it, and I want you to help me get it," said Captain Monroe, trying to hold his temper for the first time in many years.

The mermaid was unmoved.

"You have seen a mermaid, Captain, which as you well know means your days are numbered," she said. "Why waste them in fevered pursuit of gold you will not live to spend?"

Captain Monroe's teeth ground and his every muscle tensed in tandem. If any man of his crew had spoken to him the way the mermaid had, that man would have felt the back of the captain's hand at very least, but he took a deep breath and continued.

"Do you eat?" he asked.

"I eat," she said.

"Fish?" he asked.

"Sometimes," she said.

"Don't you think it's uncouth for a fish woman to eat fish?" asked the captain, with the utmost contempt.

"Why? They eat each other," she said.

The captain grew impatient. He leaned in near the mermaid's face and lowered his voice.

"Do you eat to stay alive?" he asked.

The mermaid flashed her piranha-like teeth in a grin both wide and tall. She snapped at the captain, and her teeth collided only a little way from the captain's chin. Captain Monroe jumped back but did not unlock his eyes from hers.

"I eat for pleasure and to defend what's mine," she said, in a subtle, savage tone that gave the captain the shivers.

Captain Monroe proposed a bargain to the mermaid. Not only would she give them safe passage through brackish waters and parts unknown, she would guide his crew and him to swag beyond their wildest fancies. In return, he would feed her half of his captain's rations (which were sizable and good, as galley food goes) and refrain from calling her mother names aloud.

To the captain's surprise, the mermaid agreed.

For the next two months, she ate from the captain's table and led him to half submerged wrecks and slow moving galleons, heavy and ripe for the looting.

No one on board the Nemesis knew how the mermaid was able to guide them from deep in the galley without being able to see where they were. Mr Carter and Mr Chapman, who sometimes passed the night watch arguing about such things, had their guesses. Carter thought perhaps the mermaid was overhearing conversations from passing schools of fish while Chapman thought it had to do with earth tremors and scientific what-nots that wouldn't be common knowledge for some years, yet.

All Captain Monroe and his crew knew for sure is that they were growing so wealthy, they couldn't guzzle or gamble away all their money if they tried.

And they did try.

At every port of call, they drank the best rum, they wore the best clothes and bought the attention of the prettiest women, and still, the ship's hull was filling with hoarded loot faster than they could spend it.

After about four months of this, the crew had all but forgotten their strange passenger, the mermaid, and were having quite the grandest time at reckless living.

Captain Monroe was not having the grandest time or even the second grandest. Never for a moment did he stop wanting more gold, and he resented every moment spent ashore with his crew, not sailing after treasure.

Mr Carter started to indulge daydreams of buying a little farm with Mrs Carter somewhere once he'd had enough of the pirate's life.

Mr Chapman was uneasy. He did not see endless grog, gold, or girls in store for the crew of the Nemesis in the eyes of the mermaid. He saw watery graves for every mother's son of them.

One night, he visited the captain in his quarters and said, "Captain, please let her go."

Captain Monroe could not have looked at Mr Chapman with more contempt if the captain were a eunuch and Mr Chapman a cat in heat.

"Whatever for?" he asked. "The hold's not half filled."

"And when it is filled, what will you do?" asked Mr Chapman.

"Buy a larger ship," said Captain Monroe, turning his back to Chapman as he pensively thumbed through his charts.

"Captain, the mermaid has brought us a bounty we should not have dared to ask her for, and the sea's generosity in spite of your keeping her daughter prisoner cannot last," said Mr Chapman.

"It'll last long enough," said the captain.

"How long—" said Mr Chapman, but he did not finish his thought.

The stale air of the cabin was disturbed by the rapid toll of bells and the high-pitched cry of "All hands! Secure the prisoner!"

Mr Chapman bolted out the cabin door with Captain Monroe fast on his heels. The mermaid had gotten loose from her nets and was inching toward the water with four and five men at once trying to hold her still. The creature was barely recognizable as the pale, helpless mermaid they'd seen at the home of the fisherman. This was a hurricane of arms and fins, heaving men twice her size across the deck and more than one man overboard.

Mr Chapman found his harpoon and took aim with a quick prayer for a clear shot.

"Belay that!" shouted Captain Monroe. "Crow's nest, Mr Chapman!"

Mr Chapman obeyed. He dropped his harpoon and swiftly climbed the rope netting leading to the crow's nest. He cut the ropes from up top as the captain cut the ones at the bottom. Then, with two men kneeling on each arm, three on her back, and one standing on the fins of her tail, the crew of the Nemesis were able to bind the mermaid.

When the skirmish had ended, Mr Chapman shimmied down the mast to join his shipmates. It was then that the tremulous cook explained that he had been brining shellfish for tomorrow night's supper when he heard a sad song coming from the pantry where the mermaid lay hidden. He could not help himself. He opened the closet door just for a look when she launched herself toward him with her tail, bit his shoulder, and knocked him to the ground.

Before he could stop her, she slithered over to the barrel of brine and dipped her fin into it. Seconds later, she snapped the ropes that held her arms and torso like they were made of brown paper and scrambled up to the deck where the watchmen saw her, and that is how the harrowing events on the deck began.

The cook was flogged. The ladder that led to the crow's nest was replaced. This time, the mermaid was secured not just with rope but with chains as well, and the enraged Captain Monroe had her tied to the main mast in sight of the surf but just out of its reach. Fresh rags were affixed once again in her mouth, for they now knew the fisherman had told them the truth. They would have to be careful not to allow this creature to speak or sing lest they hypnotized like the hapless cook.

Captain Monroe's quandary with the mermaid kept them sailing in circles for many days. He gave her no food and instructed those who kept the watch to shoot anyone who got within an arm's length of her.

Still, there was treasure to be had. "If not by me than by whom?" thought the captain. What's more, if he made it to shore before ridding himself of the mermaid, he'd never be able to sail again for the fear of what the malevolent waters might do to him without a hostage aboard. If he killed the mermaid or let her go now, there would be nothing to stay the furious waves, and the treasure in the hold would go right back to the waters from which he'd taken it.

Unhappily, the captain instructed Mr Chapman to feed the mermaid one raw fish each day at harpoon's point. The mermaid guided them, and the voyage continued much as it had. The sailors on the Nemesis again advanced their fortunes faster than they could spend them, and Captain Monroe repeatedly counted his share of the gold pieces, always feeling like there ought to be a little more than there was.

After several weeks of holding fast to the Florida coast, the Nemesis sailed south to the Caribbean where the captain and his shipmates found it odd that they met no ships. They had become so accustomed to plundering something every other day with the mermaid as their compass that the tranquil sea with a clear horizon behind it made Captain Monroe and his shipmates a trifle nervous.

The captain did not question the mermaid. He barely spoke to her or anyone else when there were no orders to be given.

"Is that why he's the captain? A tight pocket and a sandpaper tongue?" asked the harbor master the day they pulled into New Providence for fresh water and supplies.

"I couldn't tell you. I didn't vote for him," said Mr Carter.

"Fine ship, this. But isn't the figurehead in the wrong place?" asked the near-sighted harbor master when he caught sight of the mermaid at a distance.

"I thought that myself," said Mr Carter, "But I'm not the brave soul who's going tell the captain he's wrong. Are you?"

The harbor master asked no more questions, and they were soon on underway.

From New Providence, their course shifted from south to west. The captain chose not to go full speed through these waters to the relief of his crew. Many a famous ship had been destroyed, overturned, or lost altogether in these waters including Captain Morgan's Satisfaction and Captain Monroe's first ship, the Defiance.

Mr Chapman, having become the closest thing the mermaid had to a keeper, grew brazen enough to talk with her a little each night at feeding time. Being a curious man, he asked many questions, and the mermaid answered him, though he could never be certain she was telling him the truth. He asked where she came from and if mermaids are born or hatched or something else entirely. She said that she did not rightly remember and that for all she knew, she had always been fully grown and a part of the sea.

"I would like it very much if we were made of ripples and moonlight: the embodiment of all that makes the sea radiant," she said. "But I'm sure the truth is far less romantic."

"There are more like you?" asked Chapman.

"There are other mermaids. There are none like me," she said.

After several midnights' worth of their quiet talks, Chapman asked the mermaid if she had a name. She said she did not (at least not that humans would understand), nor did she see a need for one.

"If you must call me something," she said, "You may call me Tempest. It suits my temperament."

He could not argue, for it very much did.

Mr Chapman asked where they were going. His "Tempest" said she was taking them to wealth in such abundance, they would sink their ship if they tried to carry it all at once.

"Aren't you afraid of what the captain might do to you once the voyage is over?" he asked.

"I don't think so," she said.

"Are you afraid of anything?" he asked, in a hushed voice, lest those who would prey on such fears would hear them.

"Fear is for mortals," she said, but added, "I am not fond of the quiet or tight spaces."

Hearing this made Chapman ponder many things in silence. Had the mermaid had been singing in terror of her confinement in the galley and not to entice their cook at all? Had she meant to escape, or did she let herself get caught so she could be right where her mother the sea wanted her? Why couldn't it just rain already? Surely rainwater would give her the strength she needed to break her bonds and escape. Or was the sea somehow controlling that as well? And how could that one, lone fisherman of the coast of Cape Fear have had the strength and wherewithal to catch this mysterious fish woman that had taken nearly a ship's worth of cut-throat curs to subdue?

    Mr Chapman could not answer these questions to his own peace of mind, nor did he feel he could believe any answer the mermaid would give him should he ask her such questions. It was then that he decided it was best to call the lady "mermaid," not "Tempest," and not grow too attached to her, for whether she was the death of the Nemesis crew or they the death of her, Mr Chapman guessed she would not be with them much longer.

The coming dawn marked their third day sailing from New Providence with nothing in their sights but the water and sky. Then, sails appeared in the distance. They were not the taught sails of a flash packet in her all her glory nor the wrapped sails of a yacht on holiday. They belonged to an untidy collection of what once were stout merchant vessels and sleek war ships. These sails hung under the many flags of many colors, tattered and faded on a forest of crooked, splintered masts. As the Nemesis drew nearer, those on deck could also make out the silhouettes of proud galleons that had been smashed to pieces and long forgotten on the crests of a craggy reef.

The crew was silent when they first drew near the splintered remains of the many vessels. Then, murmurs began to spread across the deck as midshipmen, boson, and others began arguing about how many ships and pieces of ships there were. More than twenty, perhaps? But with some split in half, and some piled on top of one another, it was impossible to say.

Others of the crew (older fellows, mainly) felt utterly sober and mortal meandering around a watery graveyard such as this. Mr Carter even recognized the Hermes, a ship on which he had sailed back in his navy days.

Captain Monroe was not so sentimental. He gave orders to drop anchor and row the rest of the way in longboats. He aimed to have his men pick through the ships one at a time, starting with the nearest of these ships, the Medusa.

The first day on the reef, Captain Monroe's crew investigated each ship carefully making certain nothing of value was left behind. By noon on the third day, they had recovered so much treasure, they began throwing away flawed pearls because the quality ones were so numerous and skipping silver coins across the lagoon for all the gold ones they had found. Captain Monroe himself stayed behind with a dozen men and the mermaid all three days.

A little after noon on the fourth day, the pirates prepared to ransack a clipper ship called the Valiance. She had tried to turn away from the reef, they guessed, because she had a gash in her starboard side and was resting against the rock sideways with her nose turned up. Before they so much as figured how best to board her based on the odd angle at which she sat, Mr Carter suggested they head back to the ship and attempt to persuade the captain to set sail while the Nemesis was still light enough to remain afloat. He got no argument from the weary crew, who were by this time exhausted and a little silly. As they made their way back through the cool shadow of the Medusa, Mr Chapman whispered what the mermaid had said to Mr Carter.

" 'Such abundance as to sink the ship if we tried to carry it all,' she said. Aren't you at all worried that this might be the load here might be the one that sinks us?"

"No," said Mr Carter. "Monroe might not care much for us, but he wouldn't jeopardize the cargo. As long as it's safe, we should be safe.

The surf between them and the ship felt five leagues long, for by that time, everyone's arms were rubber due the volume of swag they hauled over the last few days. Then, without warning, the rhythm of their strokes was broken by the booming shouts of the third mate:

"You! Arse-licking, hound-raping sacks o' scum!"

The sailors whipped their heads 'round in the direction of the ship. Apparently, the excess weight had slowly sunk her to the point that her bottom now rested on a rocky ledge not far from the spiny bulk of the reef. This is not what angered the third mate. What had angered the third mate was the sight of oarsmen attempting to push the Nemesis free while Captain Monroe paced the deck. It seemed that Captain Monroe had done some cool calculations in his head regarding how much treasure he and his crew could carry versus how many ways he'd have to split that treasure. A thirteen-way split with less treasure must have appealed to him more so than a forty way split with more of it, because he had given the order to cast off without his wayward crew members.

"Sons of bitches," said Mr Carter just in time to have the bitter end of his words drown in cannon fire that sunk the boat on their starboard side.

"Back, Mateys! Row back to the Goliath for all you're worth!"

Of the three longboats with which they set out that day, two stayed afloat long enough to carry their men to cover behind the Goliath.

"Why, in God's name? We're already helpless," said the timid chaplain / reluctant rigger.

"To lighten the load. Captain must have remembered that cannon balls are heavy," said Mr Carter.

Portions of the Goliath's hull splintered around them as the gunners continued their barrage. Mr Chapman meanwhile spotted a rusty cannon that was almost pointed the right way for return fire.

"Anyone happen to have some dry powder with them?" he asked

"I do," said the cabin boy / second mate, who surrendered in haste the flask around his neck.

For want of canister and grape, the newly baptized crew of the Goliath filled Mr Chapman's cannon with doubloons and waited for the Nemesis to free herself from the reef.

"Come on, you scabs can push harder than that. What kind of pirates are you?" said Mr Chapman in a coarse whisper to his former shipmates. Mr Carter's ears began to ring. Now, amid bursts of gunfire, there were screams of anguish from this one who took shrapnel in the belly and that one who caught splinters in the eye.

At last, the Nemesis broke free of the reef with a loud scrape up her backside and sunk a full half meter lower than she had been when comfortably shelved on the rocks.

Mr Chapman put one jagged hole the bow of the Nemesis, then another just left of the stern.

The cannons stopped. The air was still, but those in the hull of the Goliath dared not look, yet. Then, came noises: a shout, several splashes, and a single shot from a pistol. When they finally peered out from their shelter in the derelict ship, the Nemesis was deserted, and the limp, twisted body of Captain Monroe hung from the mast by his ankles, apparently left to drain like a chicken.

As the crew that remained climbed into their boats and rowed away from the reef and wreckage, Mr Chapman watched spellbound as the waters overwhelmed the deck where the mermaid was still fastened to the mast. And as she felt the salty waters of home splash against her shimmering body, she broke her chains and laughed for joy when she reunited with her mother, the sea.

For a moment, Mr Chapman thought he might follow her. To what end, he did not know. But he made up his mind then and there that, when he was old and wondering about what might have happened if he had followed her, he would tell himself that no good would have come from it.

"Surviving one attempted murder per lifetime is plenty," he thought. With that, he suggested to Mr Carter that he and the rest of the sea-tossed refugees commence a leisurely row toward Panama.

About the author:

International woman of mystery Martha Jones was born American but hopes to one day recover and one day give the world a book that makes children of all ages glad for having suffered the indignity of learning to read.

You can discover more of her work by visiting her website:

https://selfwriteousness.com/

You can also follow her on Twitter, using the handle:

@SWriteousness

Selene

By Georg Isen

Long ago, in a distant barony, nestled in a deep valley, a child of great renown was born. There, sweet water nourished fields of emerald green. Fat sheep grazed lazily in the pastures. Flowers blossomed and fruit ripened. Barley swayed in the breeze, but not all shared in their good fortune.

Across the narrow sea, the land was besieged by famine and disease. Drought devastated the crops and people grew hungrier by the day. Their king was at a loss. The royal coffers were empty, and taxes were unpaid. Inevitably, war was his recourse. An armada of dark ships bearing grim-faced warriors to the coast of the land of plenty. Desperate men intent on pillage and slaughter. Relentless. Remorseless. The spring rains poured down, muddying the soil, but still they marched on. Night after night, towns fell to their swords. None could halt their rapid course. Not even the royal guard.

In the deep valley, it was early evening when the messenger arrived with the terrible news. The foreign invaders were close to the mountain pass, moving fast in the shadows of an overcast night. Before dawn, a great battle would descend upon the village, but the Lord Baron was an astute man. His men were hopelessly outnumbered. He understood that it was sheer folly to meet their enemies in open battle.

"An ambush is our wisest course," he told the village alderman. "Position the archers in the higher reaches of the mountain pass. Send the pikemen to the narrow road that leads down into the valley. There, we will lie in wait for them."

It was a risky endeavour. The night was dark, and visibility was poor. Heavy clouds veiled the moon's shining face and the Lord Baron's men were afraid. So too were the villagers. They crowded into the small streets, clutching supplies and whatever belongings they could carry.

"Be ready to retreat to the forest," the alderman told them. "And remember to keep watch over the mountains. If the Lord Baron's men should be defeated, a signal fire will be lit."

And so, they waited to learn their fate. Fearful gazes skittering from the dark mountains to the children clutching their hands. Only one household was otherwise occupied.

Towards the edge of the village, stood a humble stone house with wooden stairs leading up to an old door. Inside, a man paced nervously while the midwives clustered around his wife's bed. "Push," they cried. "You must push now! We have to get the babe to safety before our defences fail."

Sweat beaded on the brow of the young woman. She was delirious with pain, hardly able to endure more but the midwives spurred her on, driving her to heed their words. One final push and her scream echoed through the valley. A dire sound. Later, the midwives swore that the Moon herself heard the cry, and hurried to attend the birth for, at that exact moment, the clouds parted, and radiance poured forth upon the land.

In the mountain pass, flurry after flurry of arrows pierced the desperate enemies from a foreign shore. With no shelter in sight, it was a deathly trap. Even the scant few who escaped down the narrow road did not fare well. They were impaled upon a pike wall of the Lord Baron's design. None survived.

A miracle!

The messenger made haste to deliver the good news to the village, but the midwives' tongues were already wagging. "The babe is our saviour," they claimed, beginning an odd sort of frenzy that spread through the village with the speed of wildfire.

Even the alderman was affected. He officially declared the birth to be an auspicious omen and sent barrels of wine from the village stores to the people gathered in the central square. Together, they raised their mugs to the little moon maiden and celebrated their salvation. Any mention of the shrewd battle strategy of the Lord Baron or the biting steel of the arrows and pikes was immediately dismissed.

"If not for the light of the Moon and the birth of the child, we would be dead," they insisted.

Indeed, the people held fast to the belief that the sight of the newly born babe melted the heart of the Moon. Some even claimed her to be of divine origin; born of the stars and protected by God.

"She saved our wealth. We should name her Prosperita," the Merchant Guild suggested but they were shouted down by the village women who had cowered in the streets when the drums of war began to beat.

"We must call her Irene for the peace she has brought," they implored but the priests who came to bless the child disagreed.

"As a child of the Heavens, she should be known as Faith or Hope for she has shown us the power of God," they proclaimed.

The young mother listened to each, in turn, but she was not one to be easily swayed. At heart, she was a vain woman. Beauty was her sole concern. With her proud husband at her side, she smiled and pulled back the swaddling cloth to reveal the child's white, translucent skin. "Her name is Selene," she announced. "For she is as enchanting as the Moon."

Truer words were never uttered for Selene was an unusually captivating child. She was calm and restful with tranquil eyes and a quiet disposition. With each passing day, she grew lovelier. Her skin, pale and pure, seemed to glow with the light of moon, and there was a gentleness about her that was very becoming. Animals and people alike; everyone loved her but none more so than her dear mother.

Without a care for the family's meagre fortunes, the young woman bought the costliest silk thread and wove fine robes for the baby girl. A delicate china bath, a boar bristle hairbrush, a silver and ivory rattle…no expense was spared. So intent was she upon caring for Selene that she even went out into the forest, late at night, to collect the plants for the balm that kept the child's skin soft and pale.

She was not alone in her obsession either.

Every morning, the village women waited in a long line outside the stone house. Each bearing gifts of food, wool and toys, they clamoured to touch the child.

"She is a blessing to behold," they gasped, nodding in agreement to one another.

Even travelling merchants, upon hearing of the babe's shining skin and bright smile, stopped by to see her. A delightful child! When they left the valley, they carried with them the tale of her birth until her name was whispered in bustling marketplaces of towns and cities all over the kingdom.

Selene. The magical moonchild who saved the fortune of a barony.

A year passed by and then another. Beyond the mountain pass, the once small village blossomed into a thriving town. After hearing the story of Selene's miracle, people came from far and wide to settle and build new houses in the fertile valley. More fields were ploughed. More seeds were planted, and the wealth of produce burgeoned in their stores. Everyone was happy. Especially the Lord Baron. His coffers overflowed with the taxes of the many merchants vying to sell their wares in the marketplace. He could even afford to build better roads for the endless stream of travellers who came to catch a glimpse of the lovely Selene.

Her golden hair curled softly around her porcelain cheeks and the colour of her eyes deepened to a violet hue, yet her face was no lovelier than her heart. Inside, she brimmed over with kindness and love for that was all she had ever known. Beloved and admired, her pale skin was said to possess wondrous powers. And none could argue. She certainly had the most curious effect on people.

Each morning, in the market, they waited in line, taking turns to kiss her cheeks and her hands. Some whispered their troubles in her tiny ears although Selene was far too little to understand. She played with her toys in the manner of other children; oblivious to the loss of reason her mere presence inspired. The growing horde stood for hours at a time, murmuring of the glories of the moon maiden. Each day, their blathering grew more incoherent. Even Selene's mother lost her mind. Her preoccupation with attending to her daughter's beauty rendered her quite thoughtless for her own wellbeing. Eventually, she wasted away into an early grave with her husband, Selene's father, not far behind.

The girl was too young to comprehend the loss but the air of tragedy served only to enhance the legend that was gathering around her.

"The Moon is her true mother," the townsfolk told the travellers who eagerly spread the word in far off cities and towns.

"She was born of no mortal womb," they said. "The babe descended from the heavens."

It was not long before the pilgrims began to arrive, gathering in the town square on the night of the full moon to offered libations of fresh milk to Selene.

"Bless us," they prayed. "Save us."

When they left again, they claimed countless miracles in her name. Testimonies of faith that drifted back through the mountain pass to the barony, rousing the townsfolk, in turn.

"Clearly, the child is more special than we thought," they whispered to one another.

Special, indeed! No one was surprised when there was a particularly bountiful harvest that year. Selene was growing into a lively child, forever crawling and toddling her way through the town and fields. A boon for which the farmers were grateful.

"The touch of her hands and feet bestow fertility upon the soil," they claimed, forgetting completely about the abundance of good rain and temperate sunshine of the season.

Likewise, the village women were quick to overlook the scheming of the old matchmaker when Anna, the blacksmith's spinster daughter, finally married on Midwinter's Eve.

"It is not by chance," they assured the travellers and pilgrims. "Anna touched the child's golden curls under the light of the full moon."

In their eyes, Selene could do no wrong. When the small girl playfully sank her teeth into the hand of an admirer whose son soon became a successful merchant, it was not far-fetched to conclude that the girl was truly a talisman of good fortune.

The aunt who took her in after the death of her parents was certainly lucky. Her husband owned a local inn that was filled every night with travellers and pilgrims seeking an audience with the child. A bowl of soup, stirred by the girl, fetched a shilling. A price people willingly paid for the miraculous properties it was said to possess; everything from healing minor illnesses to rekindling lost passion. Some even paid a whole pound for the little moon maiden to sit upon their knees. Staring into the depths of her violet eyes was thought to bring visions of the future. Prophecies and predictions far beyond the humble offerings of the local fortune-teller.

Verily, the legend of Selene possessed a life of its own.

One fine spring evening, a year later, a pilgrim fell to her knees and pressed her cheek against the child's chest. Upon rising to her feet, she wept tears of joy and swore that she heard the voice of her long-dead father in the quiet moments between the girl's steady heartbeat.

A wondrous child, no doubt…

Selene grew up in the large house which her aunt and uncle built with their newfound wealth. Her every need was taken care of by an entourage of devoted caregivers. Following the example of her dear mother, they wove the finest silks for her dresses and went into the forest at night to collect the plants for the balm that kept her skin soft and pale. Daily, they testified to her many wondrous powers until, alas, tragedy struck again.

One by one, the caregivers succumbed to confusion and delirium. Overwhelmed by their love and admiration for the girl, they were but ghosts of the women they once were. Empty eyes stared ahead without seeing. Tongues babbled senselessly. Eventually, they forgot even their names or when to eat before wandering off to die wherever they fell. Selene's uncle too fell prey to the peculiar madness while her aunt quietly wasted away on a feather mattress in a darkened room upstairs.

The girl was heartbroken. She was a gentle soul of twelve years old; old enough to understand the pain of grief. Each loss wounded her more deeply than the one before until she could bear it no longer. "I am the curse of a foreign army, not a blessing from God." she declared, locking the front door and barring it from the inside.

Only Mabel, the orphaned servant girl, was permitted to enter. On one condition. She was never to touch her young mistress. Selene bathed herself and brushed her golden curls. She washed her own gowns and wove her own silk. She went alone into the forest at night to collect the plants for the balm that kept her skin soft and pale.

No longer did she walk through the town or in the fields. She neither stirred the daily pot of soup at the inn nor sat on the knees of those who wished to hear the voices of their deceased kin. Her childhood was over. Her toys were abandoned relics of lost innocence and there she remained, locked away in the house where her aunt and uncle died.

The travellers and pilgrims kept coming but she refused to see them. Eventually, after a year or two, they gave up. The town was quiet, quieter even after another year passed. The harvests were modest after three harsh winters and the merchants were fretful. Even the Lord Baron was alarmed. A nobleman's life was expensive, and the taxes were unpaid. He sent his chancellor to see the town alderman and together they called a folkmoot in the courtyard outside the church but still Selene refused to come out. Mabel went in her stead, defending her young mistress fiercely when accusations of neglect of duty arose.

"Please, you must understand, she is stricken with grief." Mabel begged until, eventually, the alderman agreed to be patient, but it was not a sentiment shared by other townsfolk.

Resentment was brewing in the greedy hearts of dark, secretive men. They met after midnight, deep in the forest, without care for Selene's broken heart or her fear that she was cursed to bring death to those whom she touched. Their sole concern was for the fortune of the barony if the travellers and pilgrims did not return.

"It is for the common good that we are called to action. Empty purses carry ill will," they agreed, striking a plan in the dead of night.

It was a clever scheme for Selene's sixteenth birthday was mere months away. An age when a girl was oft betrothed in those days. A bride with no groom. A sorry plight that the dark, secretive men pledged to remedy. "We shall send out messengers to every city and town in the kingdom. We shall call for the suitors of the miraculous moon maiden to come forth," they announced.

It was too late to stop them when, finally, the loyal Mabel heard the excited whispers in the marketplace two days later. The messengers had left the previous evening. There was naught to be done other than plead with the alderman for help.

"You must close the gates and turn away the suitors," Mabel cried. "My mistress has sworn to God that none shall ever see or touch her again."

But the alderman merely shrugged his shoulders. "I have no authority to close the gates," he answered. "You will have to speak to the chancellor."

The chancellor, in turn, declared that he too possessed not the power to bar the gates. "You should meet with the Lord Baron," he suggested. "Only he may issue such an order."

It was a long walk to the castle and Mabel was exhausted when she arrived, but the request for an audience from a humble serving girl fell on deaf ears. The Baron was too busy with whatever activities fill the hours of a nobleman. It was three days before he sent word that he would see her, but again it was too late.

The suitors were arriving and, for the first time in many a year, the town was festive and lively. The bards sang and the horses neighed. The children laughed and played in the courtyard outside the church while the priests heaped blessings upon the pilgrims. In the marketplace, young men, eager to make a good impression on their prospective bride, bought silk and wool from the merchants. They bought nuts and sweet fruit from the farmers before traipsing up the hill to the house where Selene's aunt and uncle died. There, they laid their gifts upon the stone stairs before the great oak door and called for Selene to come out.

"My mistress will not see you," Mabel told them but

they refused to listen.

They tied flowers and ribbons to the fence, and sang the songs that young men do when they are in love but still, Selene would not come out. The sun set and darkness fell before the suitors tired of waiting. Slowly, they made their way back down the hill to drink fragrant wine from one of the taverns before settling down to sleep in one of the rooms of the town's many inns.

By nightfall the next day, there were twice as many suitors. The day after that, thrice more. The taverns and inns were overflowing so the village women, who once cowered in the streets for fear of foreign soldiers, opened their doors to lodge the strangers who came to vie for Selene's hand in marriage.

Mabel begged them to leave but they would not listen, so she went to the church to beg for their help. "My mistress has sworn to God that none shall ever see or touch her again. Will you protect her sacred vow?" she asked but the priests were reticent to offer assistance. "All we can do is pray for her," they said and sent the serving girl on her way.

The merchants were even less helpful. Mabel asked them to band together to drive the suitors away, but they flatly refused. "We cannot chase away customers," they declared, stuffing gold coins into their bulging purses.

Likewise, the farmers declined her request. "We have families to care for," they explained, offering a few ripe tomatoes as a gift for Selene and continuing to sell their produce to the horde of hungry suitors.

The alderman was not willing to help either. He barely listened to her plea before rushing off with the chancellor to a feast at the Lord Baron's castle in celebration of the payment of overdue taxes.

Sadly, the innkeepers and tavern owners were no different. They were too busy to hear Mabel. Not even the women of the town were prepared to heed her call. They had lodgers to feed and laundry to wash.

Outside the great oak door, the bards sang, and the young men parried with swords to while away the hours, but Selene would not come out. She held true to her word until the last one left.

The young men were unhappy, but unhappier still was the town they left behind. Aside from the odd tradesman passing through, the inns and taverns were empty once more. In the marketplace, the farmers sold their produce and the merchants hawked their wares, but no one bought more than they needed.

It was a quiet town in a distant valley, not known for anything other than the miraculous babe that saved a barony, but Selene was not a child anymore and the townsfolk were no longer happy. All-day long, there was nothing but complaints. The village women wanted lodgers, and the inns and taverns wanted patrons. The farmers wanted a bountiful harvest and, after the death of his youngest son in service to the king, the Lord Baron wanted more taxes. Once again, he sent the chancellor to collect, but no one could pay and the alderman was forced to call another folkmoot.

"This is Selene's fault," the people cried. "Selfishly, she hides in that big house with no thought for our suffering."

The alderman shrugged his shoulders. Not knowing what to say, he called upon the priests who recited prayers that offered little comfort to those gathered in the courtyard outside the church that night. Helplessly, they stood there, bemoaning their fate. It was inevitable that the dark, secretive men would again be called upon to act.

They knew that Selene went out into the forest at night to collect the plants for the balm that kept her skin soft and pale.

They also knew that she would be alone.

Oh, what a sight she was to behold! The plumpness of childhood had gently curved her into the most glorious of young women. Her golden hair curled as delicately around her porcelain cheeks as they remembered, but her lips were as full and red as a blood moon. For a moment, the men forgot why they were there. Never had they seen such alluring beauty. Selene glowed from within as if her very soul was a moonbeam. Soft and pale… They longed to caress her high, rounded breasts and trace the graceful arch of her back with their fingertips, but she did not welcome their passion.

Instead, she ordered them to leave so they did what some men do to loveliness they can never possess.

They destroyed her.

They cut off her hands and her feet, but the horrors did not end there. They took her scalp; long golden curls hanging limply from bloody hands. Then they flayed every inch of her shining skin before removing her violet eyes and the gentle heart that once beat within her chest. Yet still it was not enough. One by one, they pulled out her teeth and then set about lighting a fire to boil the flesh from her bones. Only then were they satisfied. They raised their mugs of wine to celebrate their triumph and returned to the town to divide up the spoils.

The bones of the sainted moon maiden, whose birth saved a barony, were given to the priests for the pilgrims to touch as an act of faith. The deep violet eyes, said to offer glimpses of the future, went to the chancellor and alderman who had need of such knowledge to best govern the town. The Lord Baron, still in mourning for his dead son, took her gentle heart. He passed a law forbidding any noise in the castle after dark. It had to be quiet if he wished to hear the boy's sweet voice from beyond the grave. To the farmers went her flesh for compost as well as her hands and feet to bring fertility to the soil. Likewise, the teeth that once sank playfully into the hand of an admirer were awarded to the Guild to ensure the prosperity of their various tradesmen.

The women of the town were not forgotten. They took the golden curls that brought about the marriage of the blacksmith's spinster daughter and wove the silken locks into a fine veil. It was kept under lock and key until, under the light of the full moon, it was passed around for the price of a shilling to unmarried girls and widows who travelled from far and wide in the hope of finding a husband.

The shining skin, the dark and secretive men kept for themselves. They soaked it and cured it to make talismans of good fortune. Purses of Wealth. Soup Paddles of Healing. Collars of Peace. All made from the magical skin that glowed with the light of the moon for which she was named.

Selene.

Mabel fretted when her mistress did not return. Something was amiss. A fall, an animal attack, a wrong turn…it did not matter which. She had to find her, but the forest was large and difficult to negotiate, and there was no one she could turn to for help. Those who knew the way to the clearing where the plants for the skin balm grew were long-dead, yet she was determined to try. All day long, she marched on through the dense thicket. A tiring task that was not without its dangers. She twisted her ankle on a root and cut her arm on the sharp branch of a dead tree, but she pressed on, through the mulch and past the thorny bushes, until the sun set, and darkness fell. Exhausted and lost beyond any hope of finding her way, she fell to her knees.

"Mistress," she cried aloud. "Where are you?"

Later, in the years that followed, men schooled in logic and reason insisted that what happened next was a coincidence but, at that exact moment, the moon rose in the sky. Finally, the servant girl understood why Selene and her mother, and all the other women went by night to the forest. The path to the clearing could only be seen when the moonflowers bloomed.

More than once along the way, Mabel was tempted to touch the white petals with their deep violet trim. So pale and soft. They invited her caress, but she resisted the urge; remembering a warning from her long dead grandmother. "Beware of the moonflower, child" she said. "It brings only madness and death."

Alas, madness and death were what waited for her in that clearing. The torn gown that was woven from the finest silk. The bloodied axe. The large cast-iron pot used to boil the flesh from the moon maiden's bones. Mabel wept until she thought her heart might explode. Only then did rage consume her. Where were the remains of her young mistress buried? Crawling on her knees, she hammered the ground with her fists and clawed at the soil with her nails; searching for the grave that was never dug. Nothing. Only the basket that Selene used to collect plants for the skin balm.

The very sight of it made Mabel weep again. It sat, illuminated by a single moonbeam beside a young silver birch tree. Cautiously, she pulled aside the cloth that covered the plants and peered inside. There, scattered among the sprigs of lavender, dandelions and elderflowers used to soften and whiten the skin were two of the most dread witch herbs. The black cherries of nightshade, and the leaves and stem of a young moonflower plant, picked before it bloomed for the first time. Again, her late grandmother's words echoed through her mind. "Together, they are said to render a girl more lovely and captivating than the moon. And some women are vain. They care more for beauty than the danger of poisons."

Finally, the truth was revealed. The delusions, the visions, the voices from beyond the grave. It all made sense. So too did the loss of memory, the illness, and eventual death. Selene was neither the miraculous moon maiden nor the curse of a foreign army. She was the infused essence of poison. Delivered immune through the tiny doses she was steeped in from birth, her touch remained noxious and deadly to others.

It was a sad fate. The babe who was said to have saved a barony. Would her life have been different if she was named Irene for the time of peace her birth heralded? Would she have been any less enchanting if her mother prized faith, hope or even wealth above beauty? There were no answers to be found. Mabel's heart was broken. Her only consolation was the certainty that the guilty would not be difficult to find. Eventually, that which lay in the darkness of secrets and ignorance always came to light.

It was the way of Nature.

She merely had to follow the trail of madness and death, through the forest and back to the house where Selene's aunt and uncle died. There, she waited patiently, sitting on the stone stairs where the suitors once laid gifts of wool and sweet fruit.

The moon waxed and waned and waxed again but still she waited. Each night, she carefully locked the great oak door behind which Selene had hidden to protect the townsfolk from her fatal touch. In the mornings, she walked down the hill and into town as was her custom.

Not a word of warning did she utter. Not to the farmers with their foul compost or gruesome fertility charms. And not to the merchants and tradesmen who each wore one of her mistress's teeth on a golden chain around their necks. On Sundays, she went to the church and sat among the growing throng of pilgrims to watch the priests with their bones, but she said nothing. Not even during the full moon when the town's women unlocked their golden veil and passed it around for the price of a shilling. Mabel did nothing to stop them.

Likewise, she left the chancellor and alderman to sit in their chambers every morning before the day's business began, each clutching an eyeball. The Baron too remained unaware of the danger. Every night he held the rotting heart to his ear, enthralled with voices only he could hear.

Not once did Mabel accuse the dark, secretive men although, by then, she knew very well who they were. The heroes of the town! They stirred the day's soup at the local inns with their Paddles of Healing and, on Sundays, they sold Collars of Peace to the pilgrims for two ounces of gold which they kept in their Purses of Wealth. Their actions had earned her silence, she believed, secure in the knowledge that justice was being served.

A moonbeam can never be bottled, and mortal beauty does not survive death.

Ah, their precious talismans! The skin that once glowed, so pale and soft to the touch, grew black and shrivelled until it was a fearsome sight to behold.

Indeed, they were all condemned.

There was mayhem in the town in the deep valley with the sweet water and the rolling pastoral fields. Poison was in the minds of the townsfolk. Wandering aimlessly, they rambled on about strange things such as goats with wings or talking lanterns but, again, Mabel did nothing.

She sat on the stone stairs before the great oak door and watched them draw their final breaths. Aside from those who purchased the Collars of Peace, most of the travellers and pilgrims survived but the rest perished where they fell.

Word of the tragedy spread throughout the kingdom although the truth of the matter was merely one of three conflicting rumours. Most believed that a disease caused the demise of the townsfolk while others claimed that the sweet waters of the barony were poisoned by the foreign king whose warriors died on the night of Selene's birth, but Mabel cared not for their wild speculation.

She walked through the town and up to the castle, collecting all she could find of her young mistress's remains. Then, she waited until darkness revealed the moonflower path to the clearing.

Finally, she laid Selene to rest.

Afterwards, Mabel's fate remained unknown. The last of the travellers bore witness to her survival but she was never seen again. In bustling marketplaces of distant towns and cities, there were whispers that she stole the town's wealth and moved to a distant village, but those few who suspected the truth told a tale that was far more likely. They said that she deliberately succumbed to the poison and died where she buried her young mistress.

Loyal and steadfast until the end.

About the Author:

Georg Isen has long been a student of mythology, religion, folktales, ancient cultures, philosophy, and the occult arts. Under a different name, she has published numerous articles and papers in magazines, journals and anthologies. The Making: a trilogy is her first foray into the world of fiction. Together with family (including two cats), Georg lives on a Greek island in the Aegean Sea.

You can find her books on Amazon:

Invitation: The Making Book One
Heiress: The Making Book Two
Legacy: The Making Book Three

You can also follow her on Twitter, using the handle: @IsenGeorg

Urgent Tortoise
By Richard Owen Collins

Archie Wright knows his wife better than anyone. He knows that when she gets confused the whole world sees it on her face. Her nose scrunched into a hot little red ball, forehead folded over itself, while her hands ever so slightly slightly shake and her eyes turn cold and hard and capable of piercing through anything.

If he was here at this moment, instead of wallowing in bed, he might spare a chuckle at the poor young man and the sweat on his brow. The young man who only got a job at the pet shop so his mother would buy him a car, and is vastly unprepared for difficult customers like old Jill Wright, and also for life.

- What are you trying to say? Tell it like it is, boy.
- It's actually quite simple, ma'am, like I said –
- Don't "ma'am" me. I know what you're doing. Don't patronise me.

Here a list of expletives plays through her head which she manages to refrain from saying out loud. Things about how she's been alive longer than this shop and all its workers, and certainly much longer than the little boy in front of her, who hides behind his uniform and name tag and counter, whose little nostrils keep flaring the more stressed he gets, whose acne looks like it would catch fire if he heard the things old Jill is calling him in her head.

- ... I'm not sure how to explain this to you in another way.
- You haven't explained anything.
- We have three tortoises in stock. They are all infants.
- What?
- They're all babies.
- That's no good! I can't do with a baby one. He may be losing his marbles but I bet you he could still tell his old friend from a baby one. Haven't you got a fully grown one? It's got to be around the same size, or he'll notice. He may be losing his marbles but he's not gone yet.
- Like I've said many times already, ma – uh, no, I'm afraid we don't. We only have infant tortoises in the store at this moment in time.
- Can I speak to your manager?

- No.

- . . . Excuse me?

- She's not here.

- Well can I speak to a grown up then? Who's in charge of this bloody place?

- Hey, I turned eighteen two months ago.

- I'm sure your mum is proud. But you don't seem to understand me. I need a fully-grown tortoise. Today.

- I do understand. But I'm afraid I can't help you.

- You must have one! This a bloody national chain. Can't you check your stock markets or something? On this thing, the bloody computer? Isn't that what they're for? I don't know what they're for if it's not for checking.

The thinly moustached adolescent behind the counter lets out an unsubtle sigh. This furious little old lady has taken up most of his morning already. But here he will learn a valuable lesson about customer service; it is not about helping people, it is about adding enough credibility to the lies you give as reasons why you can't help them.

He nods his little head.

- Sure, I can do that for you. I'd be thrilled. Just try and stop me.

He jabs at the keyboard with his knuckles – JHCVKHBC – then waits for what feels like an appropriate number of micro-seconds. Old Jill looks at the floor and chews her upper lip. The adolescent sighs again and surprises himself by actually feeling something akin to the disappointment he is showing – probably more about the turnout of his life than his imaginary search – and shakes his little head.

- I'm overwhelmed with sorrow. But it's like I said, over and over. We only have baby tortoises.
- Well. That's not good enough now, is it?
- Can I interest you in one of the infants? They're pretty cute.
- Too bloody small! What do you think he'll say if he sees a baby one in the garden? He may be losing his marbles but I think he'll know the difference.
- . . . I honestly don't know how to answer that.
- What am I supposed to do then? He's given up, you know. Wouldn't even get out of bloody bed this morning! Now Tony's gone, it's, it's like, like he's just

given up. Sits all day in his chair, drinking his brandy, waiting to join his old friend . . . Oh, for goodness sake . . .

Old Jill wipes away the terribly rude tears that have invited themselves onto her face. The pubescent employee of the pet store feels an unexpected pang of sympathy for this old lady, and lowers his head and his voice, inviting her to come close.

- I'm not supposed to tell you this. But there's another pet shop in town. They may be able to help you.

Old Jill has to stop herself from gripping the young man's hand; the intensity in his voice seems to suggest she should.

- It's in the shady part of town, you know, where Blockbuster used to be. Here's the address.

He rips off a scrap of paper from the receipt roll. He scribbles down the name of the street where he used to go with his grandmother every Sunday for a film and chocolate. It was their little ritual, before economic crisis brought most of the business down and left only empty buildings and grandma died.

- Go, now. Who knows who's watching.

Old Jill thanks the young man no fewer than twelve times, shoves the precious note in her handbag, then leaves the pet store.

As old Jill soldiers on through the humble little Welsh valley town, she gets sentimental, like she often does, as she recalls the things her husband brought her back from his many voyages at sea. An engineer in the Royal Navy in his youth, Archie visited all parts of the world, and always made a point of finding something unique to bring home for his darling wife. Earrings from Singapore. Satin pyjamas from India. A photography collection from Malaysia. A hat from Hong Kong. Flowers from just about everywhere. A brooch from Australia and a pendant from Argentina.

In the late 1950s, Archie set sail on an expedition to the Galapagos Islands. He would be gone for six weeks. The time apart was always difficult for them, but Jill got through it by dreaming of all the things her husband would fetch for her. Her husband, the globetrotter, who made the world look small and her heart feel huge.

She pictured all sorts of things; a rare oyster pearl, an exotic, one-of-a-kind flowers, a coconut shell filled with a youth-giving elixir.

She was surprised when her husband returned home this time accompanied by a giant tortoise. He had smuggled it onto the boat and back into the country. She was at first, unimpressed. She quizzed the man on what kind of fever must have set in on the seas and what medicine he had been taking for it. He told her to shh and help him get the animal inside before anyone noticed.

- Archie. It's a tortoise.

- Yes. His name is Tony.

- Why is there a tortoise in our living room?

- I found him on the beach. He was standing there, just, staring out to sea. I sat with him for a while, and we both felt this . . . I dunno what it was. Peace. An understanding. We just listened to the sea.

- So you brought the bugger all the way back to Wales?

- What was I supposed to do?

It was decided. Despite Jill's protests, Tony would stay. Archie built a greenhouse shed in the back garden for him, while Jill complained of his madness to her friends.

But after a while, she began to understand. She saw the way the man and his shelled friend spent many silent nights together in the back garden, quietly sitting under the stars, together, content. She had never encountered a love quite like that between her husband and his tortoise. It was, in fact, almost definitely because of Tony that they never had children. Not that either of them regretted it. Jill had never felt that maternal yearning that society expected of her, and Archie had already found his heir, the giant, silent creature that was likely to outlive them both.

In many ways, Tony was better than a child. He certainly made less mess and noise than children. He didn't ask for anything, only his heated greenhouse at the bottom of the garden and the wordless company of his human friend.

That was how it was; Tony was no one's pet, he was another co-inhabitant, the third member of the marriage. And the three of them shared their life together for six consecutive decades, until, a few months ago, the old tortoise started getting sick.

They took him to all the vets they could, but no vet could save him.

When Tony died, Archie went over a cliff.

He had, as old Jill had noticed, been growing more and more forgetful in his old age, more easily confused and agitated and querulous, and the death of his best friend seemed to put a permanent puncture in his mind.

Now he no longer has the routine of feeding and sitting with his old pal to guide him through the days. All he does is sit in his chair and drink the pain away, taking his anger out on his wife, shouting at her whenever she comes near, or, even worse, refusing to look at or talk to her altogether, choosing to bury his nose in the bottle. Old Jill passes the night-time by crying, for when Tony died, her husband's spirit seemed to pass away with him, On the morning of this particular day, where Jill finds herself walking through town, looking for a tortoise to replace their old friend and hope beyond hope things can go back to normal, the bitter old man refused to even get out of bed. Jill tried her best to coax him, but it was no use. In all their years of marriage, through all their ups and downs, she has never seen him like this. Limp, defeated.

She knows the end is close, unless she can find a way to bring their old friend back.

At noon, as her soles start to burn and her joints audibly creak, she finally reaches it. The old shopping street, where she and Archie used to come every Saturday, now made up of a few kebab shops, a sex shop, and otherwise, mostly vacant buildings.

She enters. Inside is dark, the only light a low purple fluorescent beam. A shirtless man stands behind the desk, staring off into space. When old Jill enters, he is brought back into reality. Bald, goateed and covered in tattoos, to old Jill he looks like the sort of person who gets put behind bars at the end of the investigative programmes she and her husband used to watch before the lost the capacity to follow television narratives.

- Can I help you?

- Hello. I need a tortoise.

The man eyes her up suspiciously, as if he believes she has some hidden motive. He blankly gestures to the cages all around them. Spiders, scorpions, snails, snakes, eels, jellyfish, crabs, and some other animals old Jill cannot even identify.

- . . . I need a tortoise, please. And not a baby one. I need a fully grown one. Preferably at least fifty-five years old.

The bald man scratches his head, then inhales sharply, between his teeth.

- . . . Nah. Got nothing like that. Sorry, love.

Jill turns to leave. She has nowhere else to go but back home, to her dying husband, whose only illness is grief (well, and also what looks like symptoms of Alzheimer's, but as far as she is concerned if the grief can be cured then so can everything else).

- How about a terrapin?

Old Jill stops before she reaches the door and turns around.

- A what? A terror pin?

- You know. A bit like a tortoise. Smaller though.

He shows her to some terrapins, climbing over each other in their small cage. She shakes her head.

- He may be going dumb, but he's not that dumb. Not yet.

- I can get you a tortoise. Give me a week.

- I'm afraid that won't do. I need it today. He won't even get out of bed. He may not last a week.

- Oh, you need a today tortoise? Hm.

- Yes, it's an urgent tortoise.

- How about an echidna? They make for great pets.

- No, it really must be –

- You'd be surprised how affectionate some tarantulas can be.

- Heavens, no –

- I've got a baby jaguar coming in next week, you can impress all your little old lady friends.

- Terribly sorry to waste your time, but no thank you.

- Has to be a tortoise, eh?

- Yes. Yes it does. He was . . . He was our best friend. Archie's been a wreck since he left us.

The bald man bows his head in sympathy, but sympathy is not what old Jill wants, she wants a fully mature Galapagos tortoise, one whose calm, quiet presence will bring her husband back to life, and why is that so hard to find?

Her back hurts.

- Have you tried the market?

She wonders why on earth she has not thought of this already. She nods her head repeatedly.

- Oh. I didn't think.

- Tell you what love. My mate Sahin, he's a top boy. He might know how to help you. He runs the fish stall. You know it?

She is not immediately familiar with it but she reckons she can spot a man standing with a pile of fish, so she nods.

- Tell him Ricky sent you. Tell him what you need. He'll take care of you. Alright love?

She does her best to retain all the information. Sahin. Fish. Ricky. Names and places. She is tired and in pain. She wants nothing more than to sit down with a cup of tea and a mystery novel, the way she has spent her Saturday mornings for the last few decades. But she will not give up. If her mind was crumbling, due to impossible grief and sadness, Archie would not give up on her.

She may not know much, but old Jill knows this, for sure.

She thanks the shirtless bald man and heads for the market.

As she walks she lets her mind wander and it goes where it usually goes, back to warmer times.

They were on the beach. The three of them. They'd had a nice day out, walking along the promenade, eating ice cream, listening to the birds. They stopped for a while to look out at the sea. Jill took her husband's hand and asked him something.

- Do you think he ever wants to go back?

- Back? To where?

- To the sea. To home.

Archie considered this while stroking his chin. He looked to Tony, by his feet, then out to the big blue world in front of them.

- Let's see.

They walked Tony to the edge of the land, where the incoming tide brushed against their toes. They simply stood there, waiting to see what Tony would do. The married couple looked down at him, standing in between them. They could see deep thought in his old eyes.

Jill took a deep breath and asked another question.

- If he wanted to, should we let him go?

Archie said nothing. Jill knew exactly what he meant. Tony did not move. His feet stayed planted in the sand, as the waves washed over them. The three of them stayed like that, perfectly together, for a long time, until the sun started sinking into the water before them.

- Guess he knows where his home is.

Archie let out the faintest smile.

Old Jill's back is on fire by the time she reaches the marketplace. She usually avoids the bustle of this place, but today she will tolerate it. She marches her way through the vendors and their shouted offerings, through meat and fruit and clothes and pirated videos and toys and books and jewellery and wigs.

She smells the fish before she sees it.

The man at the stall is overweight, with thinning black hair, a thick moustache and a gold necklace. She walks right up to him with a disregard for her usual manners, something she is finding strangely refreshing. She has no time for pleasantries.

- Are you Sahin?

The man shows a glimmer of recognition, flicking his eyes and back forth.

- . . . No. Who's asking?

- Oh. I'm looking for Sahin. The fish man. Dicky sent me.

- Dicky?

- He runs an exotic pet shop. All sorts of foul creatures.

- Oh, you mean Ricky?

- Excuse me, yes. He sent me. He said you might be able to help me.

- What're you after?

- One tortoise please. Fully grown.

Sahin stares at the old lady blankly, unsure if he has heard correctly.

- . . . You what?

- I need a tortoise. Today.

- Ricky told you I could help you?

- He said you'd take care of me.

Sahin considers this for a few moments, looking the old lady up and down. Then he nods.

- Yeah, I think I can do something for you. A turtle, you said?

- Tortoise.

- Yeah, yeah. It won't be cheap though.

- How much?

- Well, you've got to factor in transport, labour, risk, you know, you're talking a few hundred.

- The money isn't important. Can you get it today?

- Hm. Might be a bit tough. It's gone noon already. It's an urgent tortoise you need?

- Yes. I need a tortoise. I can't go home without one. He wouldn't even get out of bed this morning. Not like him, not at all.

Sahin scratches his chin while thinking it over.

- How's tomorrow afternoon? Twenty-four hours?

This is the best offer old Jill has had all morning. Her back feels close to seizing up, the soles of her feet burn, but she can feel herself getting closer.

She silently nods her head.

- Where do I find you? Here?

- Market's closed on Sundays love, and it's bank holiday, you know, so I can meet you in the pub. The Duke. On Windsor Street, not far from here. You know it?

She can vaguely recall the establishment, from the mid-70s, when she and Archie would go there for quiz nights, when it had a different name and everyone smoked inside.

She silently nods again.

- Thank you. Thank you ever so much.
- No problem love, no problem . . . Uh, the thing is, I'm sure you understand. A job like this, unusual, short time frame, you know. The cost is up front. I'm sure you understand.
- . . . You want the money now?
- Yeah, that's the thing, for a deal like this, the cost is up front. I'll need to pay my man to get the cargo, so, you know, I need to protect myself. I'm sure you understand.
- Hmm, well . . .
- It's the only way I can help you, love.

Old Jill watches the man carefully. Her gut tells her to run, but her heart tells her this is the only chance of bringing Archie back, however slim it may look.

It is all she can do to drop her faith into the palms of this stranger.

She fetches her purse from her handbag and opens her purse.

- How much?

When old Jill gets home, exhausted, close to collapse, she finds that Archie has not moved from his spot in bed. He has spent the whole day stewing in his own despair. This is not the man she married.

She shakes him. He groans and swats at the air. His paw makes contact with her chin. She winces.

- For goodness sake, Archie.

- Get out of it. Leave me alone.

- Is this how you want to live?

- I said leave me alone.

Tears fill old Jill's eyes.

She realises she has no choice but to leave Archie, the man who has stood by her side for over sixty years, to rot in bed. She goes downstairs and pours herself a glass of milk. She is too tired to move to the living room so she sits down, right there on the kitchen floor.

Tomorrow, she tells herself. Tomorrow, it'll be okay, Arch, just you wait, wait 'til morning, Tony's coming back, I promise.

She closes her eyes and nods off right there on the kitchen floor and dreams of the stranger she has entrusted her and her husband's future with.

*

The Duke is usually quiet on Sunday mornings. Quiet enough for old Jill to easily spot who comes in through the door, and who doesn't. From her little spot in the corner, under the portrait of some noble figure, she waits, while sipping her tea, one eye on the clock. It is still possible the unsavoury man she met yesterday is late. It is still, at this point, entirely possible that he is held up in traffic, banging the steering wheel in frustration, desperate not to fail on his promise. It is not beyond reason that at any given moment now, he will rush in through the door, frantically look around, and exhale in relief when he spots his appointment, patiently waiting for him.

An hour passes. Then another. Old Jill finishes her pot of tea and stares at the floor. She is at least thankful she is sitting down and not being forced to walk around the whole town.

The pub landlord approaches and asks if she would like a refill. She declines and explains how she put her faith in the kindness of strangers and she got ruined. The landlord meekly expresses his condolences.

They aren't worth much.

Old Jill stays in her spot until the evening comes and the pub fills up. The landlord feels too bad for her to ask her to move, and she has no reason to go home. The man she loves is not there anymore, only a foul-mouthed stranger waits for her, a shell of a man who has lost his shelled friend, still stuck in his bed and in his head.

She is oblivious to the noise and people all around her. The herds of drinkers who treat going for a drink as more than a hobby. For them, the act of consuming alcohol together is a lifestyle, a status symbol.

She is thinking of ways she can finish it off and join Tony in the afterlife when a young man with a beard watches her, all alone, in the corner of the pub. The young man is getting married next week. He and his friends are out on the town, in the predatory way gangs of lads gather for mischief. The young man is curious to why an old lady would choose bank holiday night to come and sit in the corner of the pub alone and stare at the floor.

He approaches old Jill.

- Are you alright, old girl?

She half lifts her face and sees the young man, his unruly facial hair, his exposed chest, his drunken swagger. She usually avoids these people religiously, the product of corrupted and softened generations, but she has no reason to be afraid anymore, no reason to care. She shakes her head.

- What's wrong?

- . . . Honesty is dead.

- Oh. Shit.

- Language.

- Is there anything I can do to help?

- No. Thank you.

- Alright. Maybe you should get yourself home.

The young man turns around and heads back for his cluster of friends who are deep in a serious discussion about where the best gash will be tonight. Bank holiday Sundays. The best nights.

Just before the young man is out of earshot, old Jill decides something.

- I don't suppose you have a tortoise, do you?

The young man stops, presuming he has misheard.

- What's that love?

He turns around and nears her again.

- A tortoise. Do you have a tortoise?

- . . . Uh, no.

- Okay. Nevermind.

- Any particular reason, or? Just curious?

- My husband. He won't get out of bed. He's not the same, not since Tony died. He loved that tortoise.

- Oh . . . Sorry to hear that.

- What good is sorry?

- Hold on . . . Is your husband Archie Wright?

For the first time all evening, old Jill lifts her head to the world, and her eyes light up.

- Yes. Do you know him?

- Yeah, well, no, I mean, my dad did. I met him when I was a boy. The weird man with the tortoise.

- Yes, that's him!

- Yeah, everyone knows old Arch like. Hard to forget a bloke sat in the pub with a giant tortoise. Sorry to hear the old git passed away. The tortoise, I mean.

- I gave money to a strange man at the market. He said he'd find me a tortoise. He lied to me.

At this point the gang of lads have noticed their friend is in conversation with an elderly lady. Jokes are made about his standards having dropped, about his tastes maturing, things like that. One of them calls over to him, asks what on earth he is doing. The young man gives old Jill an assuring look and promises he will return. She is sick of promises.

The young man converses with his group and, after a few minutes, Jill thinks she might be crazy, but she is certain she has seen one of them before. That wispy moustache. That teenage face. Before she can place the face, the whole lot of them come over to old Jill in her spot. For a second she feels afraid, but there is no menace on their faces.

- Listen, love, we've thought about it, and we agree that there isn't a much better way of spending my stag do than by sneaking into the zoo. Don't worry. Leave it with us love. You'll have your tortoise.

Sometimes, old Jill thinks, the world is not such a terrible place to live in.

- It's got to be fully grown!

*

- Archie, it's time to wake up. Come on now. You hear me?

The old lump stirs from under the covers. Old Jill whips open the curtains and evil sunlight floods the room, and in response, a long, vengeful groan. The sky is bluer outside than it's been in a long time, old Jill is sure of it. She feels younger, bolder, and rips the blanket off the bed, revealing the shamed, hidden body of her husband, who is enraged at being dragged from his womb of self-pity.

- Get out of it woman! Damn you!
- It's morning, Arch, and Tony needs feeding.

- Leave me . . . What?

- And Gary Watkins phoned, he wants to meet you in the pub sometime soon for a catch up. You remember him? I met his son recently. Very nice young man.

Old Jill sets the cup of tea she made with a smile on her face down on the bedside. Archie rubs his eyes and looks around, as if this is the first time he has seen this room in his life.

- Gary?

- He says everyone's missed you.

- . . . Yes, Gary.

- Come on then, Tony wants feeding, or shall I do it?

- Tony . . .

- He's outside. Getting hungry.

Archie sits up and rubs his face again. Jill can see something on his face; the onrush of colour, knowledge, life. It's all coming back. As her heart is close to bursting, she kneels down and pecks the old man on the cheek, then makes her way to the door.

- Come on now. The day is waiting for you, Archie Wright.

Archie blinks somewhere between fifty and a hundred times, slowly nodding his head.

- Yes. Yes, you're right. Coming, love.

Old Jill walks down the stairs, as tears form in her eyes again.

Her husband is back.

All he needed was his old friend.

About the author:

After spending over three years travelling and teaching in Asia, Richard returned to his native UK to complete a postgraduate degree, and pursue his lifelong passion of writing. He has written short stories, articles, and an audiobook - The Dogs of Bangkok - which is available on Audible and other platforms.

Grey Gunge
By Rob Lang

Sometimes, I feel like I was born in the wrong universe. I can't exactly get away from magic, but I've always thought that there was something profoundly wrong about it. It's weird; it makes no sense; it shouldn't be there. We can manipulate it, yes, but we can't analyse it or understand it. Physics operates in parallel with it because it has to, and otherwise maintains an embarrassed silence. What magic is, is madness: pure, howling madness, bubbling up into the world from the black depths of the unknowable ontological ocean floor. You can't do anything about magic. You just have to deal with it.

The exocolony of Dumb Prince (pop. 50,000) is crammed in its entirety onto the flat top of a rock outcropping that barely clears the surface of the endless sludge sea from which it emerges. We have built right out to the edge of the available space; a solid crust sits atop the surface of the sludge, but you wouldn't want to walk too far out over it and you definitely wouldn't want to put a building on it. The atmosphere of the planet is breathable, thanks to the existence of photosynthesising microbes that live in the sludge crust. On paper we are a mining colony: that means that we operate and maintain the giant filters that strain microscopic mineral particles out of the air, and that we ship the yields in shoeboxes back Earthside through the aetheric tunnel. Life isn't so bad here in Dumb Prince--apart from the cold, the smell, the sandpaper winds, the depressing light levels, the soul-grinding cosmic remoteness, the overcrowding, the crime, the shitty food, the rationing of the shitty food, the brownouts, the administrative incompetence, the pervasive corruption and the burgeoning civil unrest. Oh yeah, and also it rains zombies. I'm not kidding.

Being a big deal in Dumb Prince is a sorry enough boast. Nonetheless, it is what I am, and one of the things that that apparently means is I have to get up at evil o'clock in the morning in order to be at the office before anybody else less important than I am. I left my apartment half asleep, my mouth tasting like toothpaste and myco-flakes; it was dawn, and freezing, and I was the only person stupid enough to be outside yet. Above the rooftops the great filters atop their columns loomed in silhouette like flyswatters of the Titans.

Sorry, it's early. I'm meeting someone important today, and we're going to save the Galaxy. What was I talking about? Oh yeah. Our undead problem appears to be closely related to the functioning of our aetheric anchor. Every exocolony has one of these: it's a magical device that stabilises the aetheric tunnel and stops our end of it from wandering disastrously out into space or down into the planetary core. Dumb Prince's is located behind six-inch steel in our City Hall; it's a sealed oak box about half a metre square, crawling with carven hieroglyphs and mounted on an iron trivet. I've seen it, once. I don't want to know what's inside it.

The thaumaturgists back Earthside seem to think that some kind of gravitational crosstalk is taking place and giving rise to the problem. This is not helpful. We have to deal with five or six thousand zombies per year, most of that in concentrated bombardments lasting a few days or a week, with a trickle of arrivals year-round. The ghouls are all unimpeachably human. They are all, of course, dead. They all get here wearing identical yellow jumpsuits that zip up at the front, and they all have name tags, written in no language we can identify using no characters that bear any discernible relation to any recorded alphabet. We have thrown entire university linguistics departments at that last problem, and they bounced off with no effect.

 Our working theory is that the zombies are somehow coming in from an adjacent universe and homing in on our aetheric anchor. Whoever the inhabitants of that other universe are, they've solved all the problems of energy draw and aetheric bandwidth whose very contemplation makes even the most brilliant magi in our one need a stiff cup of tea and a lie-down--and they're using that knowledge to send us all their unwanted biomass. The materialisations occur randomly within a large spherical volume that has the aetheric anchor at its centre; this means that about half of the zombies that come across, we never see, because they are entombed beneath the ground on arrival. The other half show up in the corresponding, roughly hemispherical volume of air that exists above the surface. Having crossed over, these specimens find themselves instantly under the jurisdiction of the local gravity, but located at altitudes that can be anything up to many hundreds of metres. Zombie-related fatalities in Dumb Prince are not common, and are as often due to impact as to bites or other infection.

Here's a nice thing for you to think about: no matter how bad things get for you, at least you're not one of those hapless jumpsuited schmucks. Who'd want to be one? Heads, you spend the rest of undead eternity in the darkness of a perfectly you-shaped cavity under the ground; tails, you experience up to a minute of extreme disorientation before becoming pavement pizza, and getting scraped up into a biohazard bag.

Sometimes, the coin lands on its edge.

#

I wasn't walking to work anymore.

The dead man at my feet was only visible from the nose upward, but he was looking at me with expressive eyebrows. Eight dead-white fingers, four on either side, poked up from the pavement around him.

I crossed the street and found a phonebox.

"Containment."

"Yeah, hi. Just wanna call one in on Upper Ozone Street."

"Singular?"

"Yup."

"What's its status?"

I looked back over at the thing, its cranium emerging from the pavement like a molehill with hair, its eight exposed fingers resembling confused worms nearby.

"Hello?" he said when I didn't answer.

"You know that one from awhile back that got here and it was in the road up to its ankles?"

He laughed. "Oh, Concrete Shoes? Yeah."

"Right, Concrete Shoes. Well, this one has itself a whole dirt overcoat, complete with concrete collar turned up to its ears. It's not going anywhere."

Someone in the background asked the dispatcher what he was laughing at.

"Partial embed," he yelled back, "can't wait to see how they tackle it." To me he said, "Thanks for your call sir, a response team will be on the scene shortly."

"Righto."

"In the meantime, we'd like you to stay where you are and direct foot-traffic around the hazard."

I groaned. "Are you serious? Its mouth is full of pavement. It isn't a hazard."

"Oh, no? What if someone trips over it? What if a dog chews it? Sir, when you let yourself forget how infectious these things are, people die. We'd like you to stay where you are, please."

I sighed. He was right. I didn't want a sprained ankle or a zombified dog on my conscience. "Fine." I hung up.

#

It got lighter, and people started to appear.

"Morning," I said to a woman as she passed me, "you should probably watch out for the, ah, yeah." She had seen it. "Bye now."

The next guy, I did a goofy grin at and said, "Mind you don't trip." He didn't seem very amused.

The response team took forever. I went up to them as they were climbing out of the van and started yelling at them.

"I've been standing here collecting dirty looks for the last forty-five minutes. What the hell happened?"

One of them was in charge and he shook his head. "Yeah, fucker of a morning. Seven cleanups since midnight. We just came from one that went through the roof of the myco-gardens. Broke both its legs on impact but it was still moving, and when we got there they were keeping it at bay with rakes. One before that, it was splattered so thinly that we were finding spots half a mile out from ground zero."

"Huh," I said, deflated. "Well, you're here now, I suppose."

"C'mon. Let's see what we got."

The two techs approached the embedded ghoul and stood over it.

"Will you look at that," said the one who was in charge.

The other one backed off a couple of paces and squatted down to get a different view. "Hey," he said, "looks like that movie poster." He came back and nudged the one who was in charge. "Doesn't it look like that movie poster?"

The one in charge stepped back himself, craning his neck to get the same angle. "Yeah," he said grinning, "yeah, it kinda does."

"You think they're gonna want the whole thing?"

"You think they're gonna give us a core drill with a bit the size of a porta-potty?"

A whispered conversation ensued, during which the one in charge glanced repeatedly down at the zombie while making vigorous horizontal sawing motions with his hand.

"Wait, wait," said the one not in charge as they were about to return to the van. "Haven't we forgotten something?" He was right. There was still one missing ingredient: they had not yet endowed their subject with a waggish codename, as per convention.

The one in charge squatted before the zombie, who looked up at him mutely. The man tilted his head to the side for a moment, pondering. One exposed top half of head. Eight protruding fingers, four on each side.

"We'll call you... Chad," he said, a grin spreading over his face. He reached out and knuckled the zombie's forehead affectionately. "Wot, no brains?"

The two techs were killing themselves on the way back to the van. They returned a moment later with cutting tools, a sheaf of biohazard bags and a tube of epoxy cement. They sawed the zombie off head and fingers at the level of the pavement, and bagged the cuttings. Then they used scoops and a little mechanical saw to excavate down about two inches of tissue, bagging what they got. That left them with nine circular depressions in the pavement, one big one and eight little ones. These they filled with epoxy cement and planed off flush.

I watched them do all this. Satisfied with their bodge, they bade me farewell, threw their gear back into their van, and drove off.

They have no idea who I am, I thought as I watched them go.

#

In Dumb Prince, if you're lucky, you live in a building made from a repurposed shipping container. If you're unlucky, you live in a shack made from slabs of crust quarried off the surface of the sludge sea. Earthside can't just send us all the building materials we want via our tunnel, because they have energy budgets to look after and aetheric bandwidth to worry about. So we build with what we have. The only exception they make is for key public buildings, and accordingly City Hall, the structure that I have the great privilege of working inside, is a swish prefab. In fact, prestige aside the build quality is terrible and my office sprang a permanent leak two weeks after I moved into it. If they'd only stick a packing crate on the lawn and put me in that instead, I would be in heaven.

"Is he here yet?" I said to my PA.

"Wow." She seemed almost admiring. "You're late."

I sighed. "You know when someone shows up at where they're supposed to be really late or harried-looking, and someone asks them, 'What happened to you?' or just stares at them, and they say, 'Don't ask,' and it's hilarious?"

"Uh, I think so?"

"This is one of those."

She shrugged. "He's here. He got bored and went for a walk."

"Thank you."

#

I found the kid in the corridor with the vending machine in it. He'd got the last can of soda, and he looked about nineteen.

"You got lucky," I said. "They fill that thing up maybe three times in a good year."

"You my guy?" he said, having a pull of the soda and shaking my hand with his free one.

"Uh-huh."

"Adonis Fish, at your service."

I laughed. "Seriously?"

He gave me a look. "Alfonso Polker? Sorry to break it to you, but yours isn't so hot either."

"Nice. You pull that out of my head?"

"No, your PA told me back there." He swigged from his soda again. "I can usually get names when I shake hands but I have to really lean in to do it, and people find it offputting."

I liked the guy already. "Call me Al."

#

"How much did they tell you?" I said as we walked.

"More or less nothing. Sorry."

Hoo-wee. "You know about the Chronoscope?"

"Yeah. They spent twenty years building it, they switched it on, it broke down after two days, and they still haven't figured out what the problem is."

I shook my head emphatically. "Uh-uh. That's just what they told everyone. It didn't break down. They shut it down, for what I guess you would call safety reasons."

"Safety reasons."

"Turns out, the future is a pretty disturbing place. Step into my office."

We stepped into my office. Fish looked around and said, "That corner is brown."

"Don't worry about that," I said. "Worry about this." I reached into the deep drawer of my desk and took out a sheaf of glossy prints. I took the elastic band off the prints and handed them to him.

He received them hesitantly. "Do I even have, like, clearance for these?"

I waved a hand. "You have clearance if I say you have clearance. Besides, they sent you didn't they?"

He turned them around and began looking at them. A lot of them, he tried rotating this way and that in both hands like broken steering wheels and still couldn't make much sense out of.

Finally he said, "Well, it's definitely hideous but I'm not really sure what I'm looking at."

I propped myself against the edge of my desk for the long haul, and cleared my throat. "From what we can tell, it's some kind of structured biomass that grows like cancer in uber-fast-forward. Super-aggressive, it replicates out of control and, ah, 'recruits' everything it comes into contact with. When we focused the Chronoscope on the future, that is what we saw. Everywhere. Naturally, the horrified seer community gave it a stupid name: 'grey gunge'.

"Look at this one." I took a glossy out from mid-sheaf and put it on top for him. "Fifteen hundred years hence: a whole planetary surface overwhelmed. The stuff is kilometres thick. Those mountain ranges you see are made of cartilage. It has horns that go out into space."

"Goddess."

"The worst stuff, they wouldn't even let me keep copies. Ten thousand years hence: objects the size of stars that are living tissue right the way through. In the latest captures they dared take, one hundred thousand years hence, parts of the starfield are occluded."

He was staring at me. "And after that?"

I shrugged. "We don't know. We can't look. Too dangerous."

"Too dangerous?"

I rubbed my neck and made a face. "Imaging the future gets weird. Paradoxes are not allowed. They are absolutely out of the question. Physics may have to cohabit with magic in our corner of the multiverse, but there are lines in the sand. That means that as soon as you look at something in the future, you make it a certainty. The images that we did capture show an

Armageddon trajectory, and the only way that we can secure wiggle room now is by keeping ourselves in the dark. Some of the seers on the Chronoscope project wanted to set the receptors to extreme range and see how it all turns out, but they got overruled. Which is good, because that would have been an absolutely terrible idea. You do that, the images that come back show a galaxy completely and irreversibly clogged up by grey gunge, and that's it. Game over, everything is doomed.

"Right now, we're only certain that it gets bad--we aren't certain that it gets hopeless. The situation might be recoverable. There might be a way our descendants can fight it and win. We don't know that the grey gunge overcomes all."

He was silent for a long time. "So you're saying... that I'm here to help you save the Galaxy."

I cleared my throat. "Yep."

"Right. And your job title-"

He was craning his neck and squinting over at the nameplate on my desk. Without following his gaze I said, "I'm the Director of Special Exobiological

Research on Dumb Prince. I share a PA with the Director of Regular Exobiological Research, and yes, before you say anything, I am the only member of my department. We've got a small contingent of scientists and thaumaturgists on this rock whose services I can generally commandeer when I need to."

He was silent again. "I just have one question."

"Go."

"Given everything you have just said: why aren't governments everywhere utilising every atom of their financial and organisational clout right now to combat this interstellar existential threat?"

I laughed at him. "Because governments are only made out of humans, and one of the most exasperating things about humans is that they tend to steeply discount the future. Especially other people's. This is not a problem that is going to affect anybody currently alive. It is not going to affect our children, or our children's children. You look at a problem like this, and sure, it chills your blood right here and right now--but there's another, deeper level on which you don't actually give a shit. You can deploy resources to combat it, but you might as well be deploying resources to combat the heat-death of the universe. Nope: much better to shut down the Chronoscope indefinitely, invent a cover story, and go on as before. Maybe grant token support to an effort at pursuing solutions, in order to assuage your conscience. You are looking at that effort: me, one brown-cornered office, one ad hoc job title, and whatever assets I can scrounge from everybody else."

Yet another long silence. I really didn't like the way he did that. "Can I sit down?" he asked eventually.

"Sure," I said. I got the chair from behind my desk and rolled it over to him. He sat down in it and I resumed the desk-edge.

"I don't even need to read your mind to know what you're going to explain to me next."

"Go on."

"You're going to explain to me, why here? Why Dumb Prince? Why this—I'm sorry, but—why this grotty office in this horrible little exocolony out in the middle of nowhere, as opposed to premises somewhere a little more salubrious, a little less parochial, a little better suited to the enormous consequence of your work?"

"You're right," I said. "That is precisely what I am going to explain to you next. You're aware of the ah, anomalous precipitation that we get around here?"

"The zombies?" He shrugged. "Sure. I've read articles about it. Dumb Prince was the answer to a quiz question on TV last month."

"You know we've had two riots already this year? The people here are starting to figure out that Earthside doesn't want us coming back through the aetheric gate. It's been six months since anyone had a return application approved. They make excuses involving mass budgets, but the actual reason is hygiene. Because this is where it begins."

"What do you mean?"

"I mean, Dumb Prince's zombies and our descendants' grey gunge infestation are connected. The former will develop into the latter."

"How do you know?"

"Because scientists and thaumaturgists have assessed the evidence. We kept them in the dark about what they were looking at, of course. But there's no question about it. Our shamblers and the future scourge of the galaxy are one and the same thing. We've run DNA sequencing, thaumaturgic resonance profiles, the works. A lot of the mechanisms are obscure to us, but there's no question about the link."

The longest silence yet. It just kept stretching.

"You finished with that soda?" I said.
"Yeah."
I picked up the office bin and held it out. He dropped the empty can into it.
"I don't think I see the problem," he said as I replaced the bin. "You know this is the point of origin, right? So wind up the colony, herd everyone back through the aetheric gate, quarantining them en masse if you have to, and the last one to leave plants a bomb on the anchor. Job done, crisis averted."
I shook my head. "You're not listening. I said no paradoxes. The crisis is not going to be averted. If we destroy the infection at its point of origin here, then it

will find another point of origin. Maybe it has multiple routes of incursion on the go at once, and this is the only one we know about. Or maybe the infection is already out there, already abroad by some mechanism that we don't understand yet, and containment is a waste of time. We take your prescription, and the crisis is still a certainty, except we've thrown away our best chance to study the problem in its embryonic stage and maybe develop a countermeasure."

He did a full rotation in the swivel chair and puffed his cheeks out. "Do I have to listen to much more of this?"

"Almost there," I said. "You'll like this last part." I picked up the remote control on the desk and pushed the button that caused the office's false end wall to open.

Fish stood up at the movement, and when he saw what the retracted wall revealed, he stayed standing.

"You keep it in your office," he said.

I shrugged. "Sometimes you just have to feed your obsessions."

The uncovered compartment was shallow, and it contained a dead woman. Her arms and legs were restrained, secured to the back wall by heavy-duty plastic manacles. A nylon bridle immobilised her head and secured a plastic mouthpiece that prevented her from biting down. Her skull was drilled into in several places, and through the holes electrodes had been inserted into her brain, trailing cables out like dreadlocks. Bolted to the wall beside her was a computerised control box. Extending from the control box was an articulating arm with a bracket at the end of it, into which a book had been placed. The arm constantly moved, tracking the undirected movement of the woman's eyeballs as her gaze wandered hither and yon. As we watched, a mechanism in the bracket turned the page for her.

"We call her BC," I said.

"BC?"

"Stands for Big Cheese. That's what Containment dubbed her when they got called to the scene of her arrival a couple of years back. We opened up the vault for routine maintenance on the aetheric anchor and found her in there, draped around it. Live captures are valuable assets whatever the circumstances, but we paid special attention to her from the start because she was obviously important."

"Why was it obvious?"

"Because her jumpsuit was a different colour. Pink instead of yellow, and significantly more ornate. Look, there are still remnants of it that the excrescences haven't destroyed."

"I don't think I like where this is going."

"We ran every test we had, gave her the works, and that's when things got really interesting. We found out that she's quite unlike all the other specimens. She isn't actually dead."

"She looks pretty dead to me."

"Oh, don't get me wrong. The infection is running riot in her body, but something is stopping it from penetrating her blood-brain barrier. Whoever she was, she's still in there, besieged and with no control of her movements, but holding the line: not a mindless zombie but a thinking and feeling person, just like us."

He looked at me hard. "I definitely don't like the way this is going."

I didn't make eye contact with him, and instead gazed at the woman--real name unknown, codename: Big Cheese. Like a pathological King Canute, she was confounding the rising tide of her disease by superhuman might of will, transcendent power of intellect, or both. The infection, denied her brain, screamed back out into the rest of her body to cause hideous tissue growth and abnormality. She was covered in abscesses and cysts, overrun by sprouting tusks and horny nodes, twisted and deformed beyond any other specimen we had yet encountered.

"We tried to make contact with her, establish communication with the intelligence trapped inside that skull. But she isn't co-operating with us. We wired her speech centres up to an external voice synthesiser, bypassing the mouth she can't control anymore. The loudspeaker is right there and she could talk to us now if she wanted to--but to this day we haven't had a single sound out of her. We thought it might be the language barrier, tried to teach her Terran from scratch--nothing. We know she can see us and hear us. I could show you reams and reams of electroencephalograph that proves it. And get this. We've measured her IQ with custom batteries of passive nonverbal tests, and it is off. The chart. She's a genius from the other side of the veil, and she must have information about the grey gunge locked away in her head, and for some reason she isn't talking to us."

"She's reading a book."

"We're careful to provide her with stimulation, because we don't want her going insane." As I spoke, the mechanism at the end of the robot arm ticked and turned the page. "She's a voracious reader."

"I guess she doesn't have much choice."

"When it became clear that she was stonewalling us I applied Earthside and got placed at the bottom of a long waiting list for a day of your time. If she doesn't want to give us the information she has in that brain, we'll have to take it from there direct."

"I knew I didn't like the way this was going."

I grinned at him. "But will you do it?"

"Of course I will. They sent me didn't they?"

"I knew I liked you."

"What is it I'm looking for?"

I shrugged. "Whatever you can find. Anything in her memory is potentially useful. We just need to get it out of there."

He shuddered, then set his shoulders and approached BC. I pressed a button on the remote and the robot arm whisked the book away. BC's eyes focused on Adonis Fish, drifted away, focused on him again, and drifted away. He got close and, responding to his proximity, she started making wordless vocalisations past the plastic mouthpiece.

He retreated again. "I'm going to have to touch her."

I keep a box of latex surgical gloves on my desk the way other people keep tissues. I held the box out for him and he plucked one. Fighting his disgust, he tugged the glove onto his right hand, approached the woman again, and this time reached out and put his palm and splayed fingers against her forehead.

Nothing happened for several seconds. Then he went rigid, and his eyes turned white.

I waited and stayed quiet. Seconds became a minute, then another and another; the silence in the office was broken only by BC's snuffles as Adonis Fish did his thing, his entire body singing with tension and his teeth grinding together audibly. Towards the end of the interaction he started producing strained moaning sounds and jerking his body around, like a man trying to wake himself from a nightmare--though the palm of his hand seemed glued to BC's forehead. Finally he produced what was close to a scream and tore himself away, drawing his hand to his breast and holding it by the wrist, like he'd been electrocuted. Sweat was pouring off him.

"Are you okay?" I asked him. His irises and pupils had returned, which I guessed ought to be reassuring.

He didn't answer me. He just stood gasping for breath, staring at the woman whose mind he had just climbed inside. I had become excited: I figured he must have got something, and that it must be dynamite. I was about to ask him if he was okay again, when he spoke. Not to me, but to BC.

"Oh," he said, "oh lady, if you had been born on this side of the veil! You would have been a sorceress of great, of extraordinary, of singular puissance!"

"Why are you talking like that?" I said.

He screwed his eyes shut, opened them wide, and started blinking tears out of them. "I'm sorry," he said. "I took a lot of her on board. It's hard to correct for."

I could tell he was struggling to think straight. "Did you get anything?"

"I got... everything," he said, peeling the glove off so he could cradle his skull with both hands.

I gave him time to collect himself, but I had to chew on two knuckles at once to master my excitement. Eventually he extended his arm and pointed hard at the woman, codename: Big Cheese. "She fought me hard," he said, "but I got what she was trying to keep from me. She is the one. It's her. It's all her. She's the, the culprit, the architect, the--the mastermind. I saw... I saw..."

What did you see? I didn't scream at him.

"...the end-state. The culmination of the grey gunge plague. A galaxy congested, packed from rim to rim with living tissue, smothering everything. Untold concentrations, inconceivable masses of biological material, breathing starlight, growing and repairing itself--a supercontinent of meat adrift in the intergalactic void. Webs of tissue strung from sun to sun; eighteen quintillion pulsing hearts; electrical impulses propagating in millennial cascades across light-years of space. The totality of this flesh represents a structured, unified system; it is organised; every square parsec of material, every cell, every atom within it serves the same ultimate purpose. It is a gargantuan life-support system for a colossal neural network. It thinks with one mind." He was still pointing. "HER mind."

He took a step toward BC. "Dumb Prince's zombies. The future Galaxy's grey gunge problem. They are one phenomenon. They are her bid for immortality. For godhood."

For a second I couldn't think of anything to say.

"She couldn't do it in her own reality," he continued. He was speaking slowly now: groping his way along thoughts that were not entirely his. "The universe from which she has come is wholly materialistic. Physics rules unchallenged, and it would have killed her masterplan at birth. So she investigated options. Radical ones. She has come here, where the rules are more flexible, more congenial to her megalomaniac designs. Her crew, her acolytes--she brought them with her, but only her fanatical inner circle knew in advance what that meant for them. That they were to cross over dead, to act as the initial vector of the infection, to lay down their own wretched flesh in the cause of their Empress's ascension."

His eyes were glazed over as he spoke, unpacking alien thoughts inside his head. "It isn't too late. Everything that she is, is still contained inside her skull. She hasn't been able to copy her brain structures out to the network yet. The network doesn't exist; the wetware is not mature, the substrate is not yet in place. Underneath Dumb Prince, the cadavers of her flock wait in the ground for the stars to be right; the biohazard middens where you dumped the pieces and the slush of her followers fester toward fruition; the ashes of the matter that you incinerated lie in the lungs of your populace, and were carried on the winds to seed the planet. But it isn't too late."

"What do we do?"

He pointed at the woman, codename: Big Cheese, again. The appellation hardly seemed adequate now. He pointed right at her forehead. "We destroy what is inside that skull. There is no backup. We can do it. We do it now, and she is vanquished. As you said, there can be no paradoxes. The tide of the grey gunge will still rise. There is no preventing that. But without her, it will be mindless. It will be analyzable; it will be predictable. The future inhabitants of the Galaxy will fight it, and it will be hard, but they will win."

I looked into his face avidly. "You mean it? We brain her, and it's done?"

"Yes."

"I have just the thing."

Suddenly there was a third voice in the room. The loudspeaker in the secret compartment had crackled into life and was putting forth words.

"It doesn't have to be that way, my friends."

I actually laughed. There was admiration in it. Empress Big Cheese had finally broken her long inscrutable silence, and was speaking to us. In Terran, of course. We had always suspected that she was clever. She had been in there all along, all right: watching, listening, letting us talk, inferring our motives even as she gave us back absolutely nothing. The voice that came out to us was hard and scratchy in timbre, and even though the pronunciation was perfect there was a subtly reptilian wheedling quality to it that I found loathsome.

"The three of us stand together at the gates of wonder," said BC. "Come with me, Alfonso and Adonis, come with me both of you. Let us join hands and ascend. We will fly across years and blossom outward through space. We will be as one, and you cannot now conceive of the wonders you would know. Think, you motes, think of what you could become and of what you could possess. You fear death, do you not? Hate the limitations of your puny bodies and your finite minds, do you not? You owe nothing to the cosmos: this cold engine that birthed you, cares not for you, and extends far beyond the reach of your power and the capacities of your understanding. There are ecstasies that you cannot imagine, spheres above and below you that yawn beyond your perceptions. You would know them, and master them. I make this offer to you and to nobody else. I will make do with one third of what I had planned to become. It is a good bargain. Join with me, my brothers. The gears of magic and matter are already in motion. There is nothing to it."

"And all we have to do is come over to you for a group hug, right?" I said. "Form a cocoon and hatch out ten thousand years hence as Olympian consciousnesses instantiated in grey gunge? I don't think so." I looked over at Fish and I could see that he backed me up. "Nope. Nice try though."

I was moving around my desk. BC said, "Then do not join me. Destroy me instead, and seize godhood alone. You can do it. You will do it. Like this." What she said next I will not reproduce here. There wasn't much of it. Three or four sentences; two or three dozen words. A child could have understood it; an idiot could have understood it. Once understood, it was impossible not to remember. I don't know why I didn't cover my ears. Maybe because Fish wasn't doing it either. What she communicated to us was simple, but there was no danger of anybody else ever figuring it out; no chance of it being discovered independently or by accident. Only an evil genius from another universe could think of it.

She finished speaking and it was done. I stopped rushing to get the gun out of the locked drawer of my desk, and instead continued very deliberately: I got the key, opened the drawer, took the weapon out, checked the magazine, chambered a round. I walked back around the desk and pointed the gun at Empress Big Cheese. Fish stood well out of my way.

"Anything else?" I asked her.

There was nothing else. She was done. The loudspeaker hissed minutely but no more words came from it.

I walked forward another step—it wouldn't do to miss. I pulled the trigger and shot BC once in the head. Her nose caved in; she convulsed violently for several seconds; then the convulsions subsided and she was still.

Neither of us said anything for a moment. At last Fish exhaled hugely, waving gunsmoke out of his face. "Hey," he laughed, "you did it. You saved the Galaxy, and all you had to do was shoot an unarmed, defenceless, restrained woman in the face."

I just looked at him.

"Why are you crying?" he said after a moment. "Hey, Al? Why are you-"

Realisation dawned in Adonis Fish's face for one second before I shot him in it. His dead body hit the floor and I looked away, wiping the tears from my cheeks with my free hand. Then I began listening.

I sidled over to the door, cracked it, and looked out. There was nobody in my outer office, my PA at lunch or off running an errand for somebody else. Further out in the building, no screams, no commotion, no raised voices, no footsteps approaching at a run. I had discharged the gun twice. Maybe people had thought I was having trouble with a filing cabinet. I felt an expression that was not even close to a smile crawl onto my face. All of a sudden I had the luck of the devil.

I closed the door and locked it. I tucked the gun into my waistband.

I had the room miked up to record all the conversations I had in it. If they were interesting I sometimes had my PA transcribe them. Now I got the cassette out of the deck. I thought about stepping on it, but that wasn't good enough. I found a cigarette lighter and used it to destroy the magnetic tape itself, pulling it off the spools and burning it to ash an inch at a time.

When that was done, I took the gun out again.

There's only one way this can go, I told myself. BC didn't say what she said because she actually wanted to help you kill and supplant her. She said it because she wanted a lever that would force you into ending yourself. She was smart. Smarter than you. If she hadn't been sure of the effect, she wouldn't have said it. Therefore there is only one way that this can go.

I paced back and forth a little. Suddenly I turned the gun around and put it in my mouth. I think I came very close to pulling the trigger, but I didn't do it. The gun came out again, and I let it hang at my side.

I mean, I said to myself, what I became wouldn't even be me, really. It would be distantly derived from what I am now, and that was all: the end product of a sequence of transformations and transcendences hundreds of thousands of years long, the nature of which I was not presently capable of conceiving. How was that not equivalent to destruction? The difference between me now and me then would be much greater than the difference between an amoeba and an angel.

I listened again. There was definitely nobody coming. That meant that I had some time.

I got the swivel chair and rolled it back to the desk. I sat down, put the gun in front of me, and began looking at it speculatively.

About the author:

Rob Lang is a writer and slacker who lives and works (neither of them particularly hard) in Cardiff, UK, spending his free time in almost endless rewrites of his own stuff. You can get his weird science-fantasy novella The Deep Land on Amazon.

Notes from an Innarian Ecologist
By David Heyman

Day 0

Weather - pleasant, with no sign of later precipitation. As you may well already know (the academy has undoubtedly been promoting it enough!) I quite recently decided to return to the field. Many have asked me why I made such a decision, giving up a comfortable life behind the writing desk. Well, I can finally reveal a little about my true motivations. An old acquaintance of mine, Doctor Marvis, recently wrote to me stating his intention to fund the expedition of a lifetime. His only caveat was that it must remain a secret until we return. Naturally, I had to tell my employer that I was leaving, and a half-truth seemed better than an outright lie. He believes he has found a vital clue as to the whereabouts of a practically mythical animal. Of course, I couldn't refuse such an opportunity, so here I am, writing in the back of a carriage as I head to our rendezvous point. I have never known Marvis to be so enigmatic, even when we were searching for the fabled lost forrest of the undying he had given me a detailed explanation of where we would be looking. Starting off like this with so little information is quite thrilling, given what we have achieved in the past.

Day 3

Weather - still rather lovely. The farometer in the carriage is showing a mild 19 farrums. Some cloud cover has formed.

I have arrived at the meeting point, though I am still not at liberty to say where that is. Doctor Marvis was quite specific in his letter that he didn't want any information about our travels leaking out before we accomplished our goals. The journey thus far has been rather uneventful. However, I did spy a wonderful family group of flashhawks yesterday, hunting just above the tree line along the road. Absolutely majestic birds really.
I won't be meeting the good Doctor until tomorrow. However, looking around this little town (if one was to be generous with the descriptive) I can't help but wonder

if others are already waiting here too. It's all so terribly exciting, I don't think I will be able to sleep at all tonight!

Day 4

Weather - much the same as yesterday. You can really feel the change of the season as we enter into Zephiros and out of Erdoris; new life is popping up around every corner.

After enjoying a rather large breakfast (you never know when your next cooked meal might be when you are out in the field!), I managed to make my way over to our meeting point. This town has a rather unique statue that celebrates its freedom from the old Empire. Again, for secrecy reasons, I cannot go into much detail, but it depicts a particular mammal chewing up a map. There was actually a fascinating cluster of moss growing on one of the brass hooves. I believe it was from the Icaris family of mosses, known for their beautiful purple stems. Sadly, I was unable to thoroughly investigate this find as I was interrupted by a young woman. She was somewhat hesitant at first but eventually asked me if I was Doctor

Marvis. Quite hilarious really, since we look nothing alike!

After explaining that I was not, in fact, Doctor Marvis but one of his colleagues, she introduced herself as Doctor Luessa. It was very much my turn to be red in the face! Imagine, me, not recognising, dare I say it, my favourite author on the subject of endangered pigmy gripes. I'm just disappointed I didn't have my copy of her thesis with me. It would have been lovely to get it signed.

We sat around by the statue for some time, waiting for Marvis to arrive. Naturally, we discussed and speculated upon the nature of our journey to pass the time. Sadly she too had no idea as to the specifics of what we would be looking for. Neither did the other chap who joined us about an hour later. He introduced himself as one Mr Tardish. Apparently, he is something of a famous hunter and trader back in Ibram. Can't say I approve of his vocation, but it does make sense to have someone like him about when venturing after the unknown and exotic. I heard a rumour that the botanist, Vanessa Schmark, insisted on an armed guard on every expedition ever since the tragic death of her field partner. The singing daisy is a most terrible thing. Anyway, I digress.

We waited until well after a respectable lunchtime before collectively deciding that getting something to eat wouldn't go amiss. We returned to the meeting spot with our bellies full, and once again in high spirits. Upon our arrival we found the good Doctor waiting for us. He quickly led us away from the square and into his own lodgings a few streets away, not saying a word of a greeting as he did so. Finally, when he was satisfied with the situation, he properly introduced himself to the others. Without waiting for the formalities to be returned, he began talking about packing up and leaving! Can you believe it? I've never seen a man in such a rush before. That said, we agreed that it would be best to get moving and, as I write this, we are all sitting in a little rented coach, heading off along the old forest road.

Day 4

The first drops of rain have fallen, but it remains mild weather overall.

The coach ride has been a little tense if I am being honest. Marvis keeps glaring at me every time I try to update this journal. Not really sure what is wrong, but will add more later when I have a bit of privacy.

Day 6

A little foggy today, though still not all that cold.

Sorry to keep you in suspense, but under the watchful and apparently judgemental eye of Doctor Marvis I was unable to write any more before now. We have since made camp, and the others are sleeping, so this seemed like an excellent opportunity.

We left the coach behind a little earlier today at the edge of some dense mixed forestry and unhitched the trail donkey that had been following behind. The Doctor has, of course, been leading the way, though he seems to be doing so without a map or any navigation equipment.

We are by and large still none the wiser on the true nature of our journey, and it is starting to make me feel a little nervous. When pressed for answers, Marvis simply stated that it would be well worth it if we 'just trusted him'. Since we are now rather far away from any form of civilisation, and he is the only one with a map of this area, (I would have brought my own but obviously had no idea where we were going!) staying seemed to be the best choice. While I am technically on watch, I must confess to being a little distracted by the sounds of a cerakka calling out to its pack. While a common enough mammal in the more southern parts of the country, it is rather unusual to see them so far, well, here. Since they only really hunt small rodents and the like, I will not be bothering to wake the others. Still, I am sure they will be interested to hear about this unusual migration in the morning!

Day 7

The weather has been somewhat mixed, starting with a little rain but improving over the day.

I was, apparently, overly optimistic about my companions interest in the cerakkas. Aside from Doctor Luessa who expressed a mild interest in trying to find the group, the others were firmly against it. While I generally prefer to avoid any character slurring, Doctor Marvis was downright rude about the whole thing, saying I needed to remain focused on our mission. I reminded him that we didn't actually know what that was yet, but he stormed off in a huff instead of answering. I know it has been some time since we last worked together, but I genuinely do not recognise the man anymore.

When he eventually calmed down and returned to our little camp, he ordered us to get moving again. I would like to say that at this point I refused to continue on this rough trek. Alas, I am still to figure out how to make my own way home. As soon as I do, I will be leaving this disaster of an expedition behind!

Doctor Luessa also seems to be unsure of our current situation, saying very little to anyone actually. Only Mr

Tardish seems unfussed about our pace or directness. It feels as though we covered nearly ten spans today, heading ever further north. Only a quick break for lunch, at my insistence, gave us any time to rest.

Day 9

We experienced some pink rain today, not a good sign but I have heard of worse happening in these parts.

My fears were all but confirmed yesterday as we continued to relentlessly head further north. I no longer care for Doctor Marvis' wishes to keep this all a secret, for he is marching us right into Tajikia!

Why he is in such a rush to surely kill us all, I have no idea. I discussed my concerns with Doctor Luessa, but she has become almost excited by the idea. In a reversal of roles, Mr Tardish seems practically as nervous as I am. My personal supplies are no longer enough to return alone, even if I was now lucky enough to stumble upon the path home. Doctor Marvis, whether through paranoia or design, has started to only give out enough food for the current meal. The rest remains firmly upon our mules' back, guarded by the seemingly constant watch of Doctor Marvis. While I could try to forage for sustenance, I do not think I can trust this landscape to be entirely edible for quite some distance. Not unless I fancy growing some extra limbs or horns, and that's if I am lucky!

I will give it one more day to see if our course changes at all. If not, I will have to confront Doctor Marvis once more and force him to explain what is happening.

Day 10

The weather has suddenly become quite pleasant, much unlike our mood.

We were practically at the border of Tajikia, easily noted by the drastic change of landscape from lush forest to a thick layer of ice and snow. There were some trees in the distance, which appeared to be howling at the sky.

Before I had a chance to confront Marvis, as I had intended, Mr Tardish stopped our group. He said that he would not go another step unless the Doctor informed us as to why we were in this 'accursed place'. Disappointingly, Marvis stuck to his tale of expected glory, though still failed to provide any actual details. When Mr Tardish expressed in slightly rougher language than I care to repeat, that that wasn't good enough, Marvis shrugged and said that it would be his loss. Before any further discussion could be had, he led our pack mule onto the snow. It was morbidly fascinating to note that the snow turned black under their feet, as though this was some delicate membrane being bruised as they walked over it.

Doctor Luessa was already following him before I could even start to suggest we prepared for a return trek. I had imagined that if all three of us stayed back, then Marvis would have no choice but to reconsider his reckless course.

This left Mr Tardish and I to debate our own course of action, both painfully aware of how insane we would have to be to follow yet conscious of the fact that our food was also walking off into the distance.

I can now confirm, with much regret, that the fabled wailing iron trees of Tajikia are not an exaggerated myth.

Day 12??

The weather is, well, bloody strange. A fog was up in the afternoon that sparkled like a diamond and moved almost lazily across the land. It was confined to an area of about five lengths and notably left a shredded path of snow behind it, along with the scattered remains of at least one tree. The nights and days feel off somehow, as though the day is longer than the usual fifteen turns. Unfortunately, I did not bring my chronometer and cannot confirm this.

Doctor Marvis has become almost fanatical in his demeanour, convinced that we are mere moments away from the discovery of a lifetime. Doctor Luessa is faring little better and seems to be wholeheartedly invested, though I have no idea why. I can only speculate that she has bought into the delusion that there will be a great deal of fame to be found upon our success. At this point

I will be happy to return with most of my limbs in the correct place and shape. Mr Tardish and I have exchanged the odd weary glance, but have kept our continued general discomfort to ourselves. If would be all too easy for someone to have an accident out here.

I must confess, though, for all the terrifying oddities, there is a certain beauty to its strangeness. It is as likely to enchant you as it is to maim you if approached carelessly. Even the relationship between predator and prey seems fluid here. I saw something resembling a bluetuft dive out of the sky, attempting to snatch a butterfly, only for the bird to end up in bloody pieces on the ground. All the while, the butterfly gently continued about its business, the sunlight glinting off what I can only assume to be shards of metal in its wings. I was not willing to get close enough to investigate in this case.

Day 15??
We have finally stopped. Doctor Marvis is convinced that the series of caves before us is the final hiding place of one of the rarest animals in all Innar. Now we face

the 'simple task' of finding out which of the foreboding recesses conceals our prize.

It was at this critical point that Doctor Marvis finally deemed us worthy enough to be informed of our 'mission'. I really shouldn't have been surprised, after all, he had tricked us into Tajikia. He had walked us through the singularly most dangerous landscape in all of Caer Innar without a care for us or our wellbeing. Yet, even after all this, he managed to surprise me once more with his callous insanity. Lesser-spotted purple murder toad. I felt sick just hearing the words tumble from his mouth as though it meant nothing. He had brought us all here to die, apparently and we expressed as much. Even Doctor Luessa, with her apparent excitement of exploring Tajikia, flew off the rail when she heard what we were chasing. Doctor Marvis said nothing but reached for something within his satchel. I honestly don't recall what it was, but all fight suddenly left me and I vaguely remember thinking that maybe it wasn't such a bad idea after all.

I am afraid that what happened next was a bit of a blur for me. I do not know what magic Marvis used, but I am confident that it was. I suddenly found myself within one of the caves and equipped with some sort of ocular device and a mask that covered most of my face. The others seemed equally confused by our situation, looking around frantically to get our bearings. Everything was dark, aside from the dim luminations provided by Doctor Marvis and the spark stick he was holding. Once we had enough of our wits about us, he curtly informed us that it was getting rather late and he was feeling tired. We were apparently to make camp for the night and he would 'appreciate no argument on the matter'.

Mr Tardish was the first to voice his displeasure but was strangely silenced when Marvis held out his hand. He continued to inform us that Doctor Luessa would be taking the first watch and advised her to leave the mask on. Apparently, I was to take the second watch.

Day 15, night.

I was awoken for my watch by a teary-eyed Doctor Luessa. I would have asked her what was wrong, but given our situation, the question seemed somewhat moot. I gave her what I hoped to be a reassuring nod, and began my vigil over our crude campsite. In the silence of the cave I began to wonder if my hesitations about leaving this venture had been entirely my own. Perhaps Doctor Marvis had been using his newfound powers to manipulate us from the moment of our meeting.

Either way, it was too late for us now. I feel that this journal is less of a documentation of an adventure and more of a forewarning to anyone who finds it upon our almost inevitable deaths. I can but hope that the legends of how the toads' victims die are greatly exaggerated.

Day 16

Whatever power Marvis has over us has been relaxed, for I feel myself returning to my full senses. Likely he understands that even if we wanted to, there was no way for us to escape without him now.

Breakfast was a tense silence. Mr Tardish spent most of it glaring at Doctor Marvis, but, unlike our quarry, his looks couldn't kill. Further adding to the surrealness of our situation, Marvis appeared to be in excellent spirits. He seemed genuinely confused as to why we were so upset with him. I attempted to explain that we would die before we could make our discovery known and he laughed. Apparently, the masks he had provided us with would protect us. To say I was sceptical would be polite. However, since he was finally sharing information, I continued to ask questions. I wanted to know why he had brought us along since he clearly knew where he was going, what he was looking for and how to survive the encounter. He answered that he needed reliable witnesses, and we were the best he could think of for our respective fields. I had to concede that few sane minds would believe his account alone.

When breakfast was done, we cleaned up and continued further into the cave. We could hear them now, an ominous echo of ribbits. I must apologise for the quality of my writing right now, but I am making these notes as we walk for fear that I will not have the chance to do so later. The thoughts of turning back still linger in my mind, while Marvis appears to be focused on other matters, but these ideas are quickly dashed by the knowledge that I do not know the way, and am just as likely to run into a nest of toads as I am to escape.

The sounds are getting louder now, almost unbearably so. I wonder if this is just one or a whole nest. Legends vary as to the size and description of the creature, so I genuinely have no idea as to what will bring our deaths today. My only comfort is that I have lived a long and exciting life, though I pity my friends who will have to speculate as to why I disappeared.
Judging from the intensity of the sound, I believe we are only a few steps away from the creatures.

I can't believe it! The masks work! Thank the Source for that! While I do not approve of his methods, Doctor Marvis was not wrong when he said this would be the discovery of a lifetime! The creatures are quite unique,

*Apologies dear reader, but for reasons that will later become apparent I made the difficult decision to erase my description of the lesser-spotted purple murder toad for your own safety.

Naturally, Marvis wants to recover a specimen to bring back to the academy and has asked Mr Tardish to do the honours. Though clearly reluctant, and I cannot blame him for that, he is slowly reaching down to grab one and

Day??

I no longer know the date, though we have left the caves long behind us. It is a struggle to continue to write now, but the activity helps to settle my mind somewhat. There are just three of us now, may Erdas watch over Mr Tardish. Never, and I really cannot stress this enough, ever touch a Lesser-spotted purple murder toad. Even with gloves, the poison was potent enough to cause the poor man to explode into a purple mist. Presumable the material delayed the reaction, giving him enough time to put the creature into a bag before it happened. Even now, I am in shock. Marvis seems almost unaffected and carefully retrieved the bag with a metal rod.

We have retraced our steps and are once again close to the border of Tajikia. It should be only a few more days before we are back in the forest and then able to secure proper transportation. In our resting moments, I have noticed Marvis attempting to sketch the creatures. I do not understand how my old friend has become so callous, but I fully intend to have him arrested once we return home.

Day: Exit from the caves +4

We were so close to leaving this nightmare behind us. Yet here I am, mourning the loss of another member of this ill-fated party. These creatures, as marvellous as they are, and truly, from a biological perspective, they are easily some of the most magnificent examples of life in all of Innar. Magnificent but entirely lethal in ways we hadn't even considered before now. At least not considered by anyone other than Marvis. As I had mentioned before, he had been attempting to carefully draw the creature. What had failed to register with me as anything beyond a scientific quirk (we always like to wear our safety equipment when working!), was the fact that he continued to wear his goggles while drawing.

Yesterday, Doctor Luessa was apparently interested in Marvis' drawings of the toads. I spotted her glancing over his shoulder while he worked. His rage was unbelievable, leaping into the air and knocking her away. At first, it seemed an incredible overreaction, but in hindsight, it was too little too late. Her screams echoed through the forest while she clawed at her eyes, leaving her face a ruined mess. We tried to restrain her, tend to the self-inflicted wounds but to no avail. Everything returned to silence when moments later, her wailing suddenly ceased, and she breathed her last.

Marvis seemed more upset that I am now the only witness to our success, rather than at the senseless loss of another brilliant mind. He barked a warning at me to never look at the animal or anything to do with the animal without the goggles. A warning that should have been given to us all days ago. He wouldn't even wait for us to bury Luessa, packing up his kit and walking on before she was even cold on the floor.

Why this even happened is beyond me, how can a picture kill someone? Unless... unless the very shape and markings of this unique creature are the secret behind its lethality. I've heard of inscriptions being filled with Source, unleashing their power upon observation. Could this be a naturally occurring phenomenon?

I have put on my goggles once more and carefully deleted my previous entry describing the creatures. I fear that even if this is not lethal in its own right, the symbols could be used for nefarious means.

Day: Exit from the caves +8

I recognise this part of the forest now, we are perhaps a couple of days away from the road and a half cycle from our starting point. Maris has shown nothing but pride in our expedition. When he does talk, it is of how he will be remembered. He has started referring to himself as the 'man who solved the secrets of the north'.

Marvis even began to suggest that these animals could be weaponised, that we could make a return journey to collect more and sell them to the highest bidding military.

At that moment, I knew I could not allow him to continue. I would ask for your forgiveness, for even though I know in my heart that what I would do would be necessary, in truth, it would leave me no better than him.

Day: Exit from the caves +9

I am alone now.

I will be turning myself in to the local authorities as soon as I return to civilisation. I have destroyed everything, including the hapless toad, in our campfire for fear of what others like Marvis might do with it. I have kept this journal alone, and I hope that my notes on this 'expedition' will be preserved so that they may be a warning to others who might go seeking this folly. The beasts are real, but only death and madness lie that way.

About the author:

David Heyman is a writer based in Shizuoka, Japan. Originally from London, he moved to Japan to teach English after living in Wales for fifteen years. When not educating others about the glorious (read as confusing) English language he finds time to write. While in Japan he met his wonderful and supportive wife and now spends most of his free time with her, either gardening or generally being geeky together.

You can find his novels and short stories on Amazon:

Escaping Fiction (A World Within Worlds Book 1)

The Woman in Blue

Valentine Remade

You can also follow him on Twitter, using the handle: @minds_press

Printed in Great Britain
by Amazon